"Who was he, this other man?"

Charlotte could feel beads of sweat breaking out on her forehead. Would he ever stop this remorseless inquisition?

"Well," Jude demanded, "was it someone local? Someone I knew?"

"No! I mean, you don't know him. Look—" anger swelled her voice "—it's nothing to do with you. Leave it."

"Why didn't you marry him?"

She hesitated. "It didn't work out, that's all." She was extemporizing wildly. "I thought I loved him, but I realized very soon that I was wrong, and—"

Jude shook his head disbelievingly. "You threw Simon over for a passing fancy. Killed him," he said savagely, "for a mere infatuation." He broke off abruptly, then continued, his voice unsteady. "I thought I knew you, Charlotte. I thought you cared about us all."

The pain in his voice was lacerating her. Somehow she had to stop him from punishing them both.

RACHEL FORD was born in Coventry, descended from a long line of Warwickshire farmers. She met her husband at Birmingham University, and he is now a principal lecturer in a polytechnic school. Rachel and her husband both taught school in the West Indies for several years after their marriage and have had fabulous holidays in Mexico, Venezuela and Ecuador during revolutions and coups! Their two daughters were born in England. After stints as a teacher and information guide, Rachel took up writing, which she really enjoys doing the most—first children's and girls' stories, and finally romance novels.

RACHEL FORD

a shadowed love

Harlequin Books

TORONTO • NEW YORK • LONDON
AMSTERDAM • PARIS • SYDNEY • HAMBURG
STOCKHOLM • ATHENS • TOKYO • MILAN

Harlequin Presents first edition April 1989
ISBN 0-373-11160-6

Original hardcover edition published in 1988
by Mills & Boon Limited

CHAPTER ONE

CHARLOTTE did not reply at once. Only when the woman repeated her question did she reluctantly turn her head.

'Yes, Mrs Tarrant,' she said slowly, 'you're quite right. That's Jude Renton.'

She glanced at the rapt, almost awed faces of her small group of tourists and a faintly ironic smile flitted across her lips, to be replaced immediately by her friendly though impersonal professional expression.

It's all right, he's real, she felt like saying. But then, she asked herself, was that strictly true? Could Jude be quite real, after all the years of fame and adulation?

Since his arrival in Stratford-upon-Avon to play a season at the Royal Shakespeare Theatre, she had quite consciously taken great pains to avoid those parts of town where she might encounter him, and only now, for the first time since the motley procession of local dignitaries, ambassadors and actors gathered for the annual celebration of Shakespeare's birthday, had wound its way into Bridge Street did she allow her eyes to cross the crowded street.

He stood, head and shoulders above those around him, looking up at the flag which he had just unfurled and which was now fluttering madly in the gusting late-April breeze. His face was deeply tanned—of course, he spent most of his time in California these days. That fulsome Sunday supplement feature that she had forced herself to read—what had it said? ' ...Jude Renton, pictured with his current glamorous companion and co-star,

5

Claudia Wexford, at his magnificent neo-classical mansion overlooking the Pacific...' Though this new, neo-classical Jude, Charlotte had realised as she studied the photograph with a painful intensity, had retained every last atom of that air of ironic detachment, only just falling short of arrogance, which she remembered so well.

As she watched, he impatiently brushed back his unruly black hair, and at the familiar gesture a sharp spasm hit her squarely in her midriff, like a blow from a fist, so that she caught her breath, her hands clenching in her jacket pockets.

He shot a sardonic grin at the man beside him— another actor, whom she half recognised—then, as she still watched, quite unable now to tear her eyes from him, he said something—no doubt highly out of keeping with the solemnity of the occasion—and they both laughed, then hastily smoothed the smiles away. At least he was appropriately dressed, she thought, his beautifully cut morning suit showing off to perfection the lean, hard lines of his body. No one would ever have got him into such an outfit in the old days, though. A brief smile flickered across Charlotte's face at the sudden, vivid memory of the perpetually casual, jeans-clad drama student.

'Well, I just can't wait to tell my granddaughter that I've seen Jude Renton in the flesh!' Mrs Tarrant was chattering happily on. 'She's real nuts about him—keeps his signed picture beside her bed!'

Another member of the group chipped in, 'I saw his latest movie three times before we left for Europe. Have you seen it, Miss Mercer? He's a wow—so sexy!'

All the ladies tittered appreciatively, but Charlotte blurted out, 'No, I haven't.' Then, conscious of her brusque tone, she added more mildly, 'I've been too busy lately, but I remember all the critics raved about it.'

In fact, she thought, she'd only seen Jude's first film. She had gone, fearfully, yet hoping that by some miracle the sight of his impersonal face on the screen might exorcise all the heartbreak and pain of his leaving. But of course it hadn't. In the warm, anonymous darkness of the cinema, she had cried, even through that famous, hilarious car chase, quite unable to stop herself, until, conscious of the curious glances of the people on either side of her, she had stumbled along the row to find refuge in the deserted ladies' cloakroom. There she had leaned against a washbasin, trying to persuade the swollen-eyed stranger in the glass that she was weeping only because she was still weak from her illness. All the same, though, she had never been to any of Jude's later films...

The band was striking up, as though to entice a military precision from the dignitaries, the men in neutral morning dress or flowing national robes, the women in colourful silk dresses and flowery hats. But if that was the aim, it was unsuccessful, for most of them were shambling off in a very unmilitary manner.

Charlotte began solicitously shepherding her elderly flock away from the seething crowds. They were a nice little bunch, she thought—anxious only to see everything there was to be seen. She smiled at them.

'Let's go further along, shall we, then we can meet up with the procession again after they leave the Birthplace.'

Almost too soon, the band could be heard approaching once more, and at the thought of seeing Jude again, she had momentarily an almost irresistible impulse to abandon her group and melt away down one of the side streets—but that was ridiculous. For heaven's sake, she told herself angrily, just pull yourself together, will you? Seven years. It's been seven years since that last, unbearable meeting in the churchyard seared itself for ever into your mind, like a red-hot iron into flesh. And after the things that were said, what makes you think he'll be one jot more anxious to renew the acquaintance than you? Too many painful memories, haunting memories that simply would not go away...

Jude was level with them again, walking with that casual, almost animal self-assurance, now so much admired as part of his actor's persona, but which, Charlotte knew, was as natural to him as breathing. Oblivious of the nudges and looks of open adulation, his eyes lazily raked over the crowded pavement, as though seeking familiar faces, and Charlotte, in spite of the fact that she had deliberately camouflaged herself behind a very tall policeman, shrank back even further in sudden terror, as his gaze flickered momentarily across her face. Although she felt nothing for him now, of course, she simply could not bear to risk seeing again that look of cold, implacable hostility...

She bent her head and, delving into the brightly-coloured plastic bag she was carrying, fished out the half dozen small posies of daffodils and rosemary sprigs which her grandmother had made up for her earlier that morning.

'But can we really join in the procession?' asked one of the old ladies delightedly.

Charlotte smiled at her as she handed her a posy. 'Of course. We all tag on the end. Look, there's a gap. Let's go!'

Once hidden among the shuffling line, she relaxed her guard slightly. Jude was a long way ahead; at every turn of the procession she caught sight of his broad shoulders and the back of his head, the dark, thick hair surely shorter than it had been seven years previously, and cut square across his neck now. That once beloved head...

She involuntarily closed her eyes for a second, her throat tight. What in the world was she doing here? Debbie, the girl whom she and Stuart were training, the first of many staff, they hoped, in their new venture— Debbie would have coped perfectly adequately with the task of shepherding around six elderly American ladies for a couple of hours on the Birthday morning. But no, she had wilfully chosen to act as escort herself, giving up what should have been her first free Saturday for weeks, with the chance of a lie-in, then a leisurely bath and a day pottering about her tiny flat, at last perhaps sorting out the boxes which were still waiting to be unpacked weeks after she and Stuart had arrived in Stratford.

She had chosen, instead, almost with a sense of fatalism, to go to the very event where she would be totally unable to avoid seeing Jude. It was almost as though she had done it deliberately. Of course you did it deliberately, she thought scornfully. In the end, you had to see him again, didn't you? So what now? Well, she *had* seen him, and could now reassure herself that, apart from that first momentary twinge, which, after all, was perfectly understandable, and was no more than the wince when one bit unexpectedly on a bad tooth, she felt nothing, absolutely nothing—she was totally indifferent to him.

All the same, she was very relieved when, the procession finally having snaked its way through Holy Trinity Church, and her group of ladies, faces glowing, had handed in their posies at the altar rail, beneath the faintly ironic marble gaze of Shakespeare's bust, she was able to deposit them safely back at their hotel in time for lunch.

Now she would just walk round to their small back-street office, check with Debbie that nothing had cropped up and then maybe she would still take the rest of the day off, although Stuart might well grumble if he was there. He really did not seem to appreciate that, even if he was a workaholic, she had been feeling increasingly in need of the odd few hours' break.

Since she had returned to Stratford just after Christmas with Stuart, life had been a perpetual whirlwind of activity—exhilarating but also unremitting, both of them driven by his obsessive ambition. He had been her immediate boss in the large travel firm in London where she had worked for six years. After fleeing to the welcome facelessness of the city a few months after her eighteenth birthday, Charlotte had taken a secretarial course, then got a job at the agency.

Her sunny temper masked a quiet firmness, and though very young, she quickly became adept at dealing with people in the mass; people who were fractious, tired, awkward; people who were hysterical because they had mislaid their passports, tickets, wallets, cheque cards, luggage, husbands, wives. The permutations, she soon discovered, were endless, but she learned to deal with all the huge and tiny personal crises, with kind, even gentle efficiency.

But gradually the job, congenial and excellently paid as it was, had begun to go stale on her, so when Stuart had put to her the proposition that together they start a small tourist concern in Stratford-upon-Avon, a town only a few miles from the village where she had grown up, the challenge was irresistible. Only occasionally, when she lay awake in the early hours—a habit which seemed to have grown on her lately—had she asked herself if perhaps this had not, after all, been the wisest thing to do. But Jude Renton was far away, making one cult movie after another.

Charlotte smiled wryly to herself, remembering vividly that cold, snowy morning when, hurrying to work, she had been brought up short by the newspaper poster in the market square. 'Local Boy Returns to Theatre.' She had stopped dead, oblivious of the jostling crowds, then very slowly fumbled in her purse for change to buy a paper and read, as she had known by some dreadful instinct she would, how Jude Renton, after his dazzlingly meteoric rise to stardom, etc, etc, was about to commence a season at Stratford...

Smothering the wild impulse to turn tail and flee at once back to London, she had forced herself somehow to read on calmly. '...where his career began eight years ago, in the traditional spear-carrying roles, before he shot to prominence as one of the Dromio twins in *The Comedy of Errors*, the other role being taken by Simon Renton, his twin brother, who was only months later so tragically killed in a car crash...'

Charlotte shivered suddenly. The bright April sun had retreated behind leaden clouds and the wind was bitter. She felt chilled all through; it must be from standing around so long waiting for the procession.

Still, the sight of the office ahead warmed her with a small glow of pride. True, it was very small and in a narrow side street—Stuart was already talking about moving out to a more prestigious address nearer to the town centre—but none the less the place looked very smart in its sparkling livery of chrome yellow and white paintwork. There was a window box and a couple of tubs, filled just now with early tulips, and above, in gilt writing, the name which she had suggested and which, after long argument, Stuart had grudgingly agreed to— 'Anything Goes', which, as she had explained, gave exactly the right feeling that here was a firm which would do—anything. As well as the conventional tourist services, they aimed to make their name by being prepared to fulfil the most off-beat of demands. Earlier that week Charlotte had spent several hours tucked away in the town's reference library researching local superstitions in preparation for a Japanese professor who had requested a custom-built tour for one, on witchcraft legends of Shakespeare-land, for which he would be paying very handsomely.

As she went up the couple of steps, the door opened sharply.

'So you're here at last! For God's sake, where have you been?' Stuart's normally pale face was pink with annoyance.

'There was no hurry, surely? The procession took even longer than usual this year and by the time I'd walked them back to their hotel——'

'For crying out loud! You walked them back to their hotel!'

'Well, they were all quite old.' Charlotte's voice was placatory. She knew she sounded defensive, but with Stu that was often the easiest way to handle his temper.

'So what? We're not running a nursery for geriatrics. They paid for you to escort them round town for a couple of hours, that's all. If you're going to start using the firm's time——'

'Oh, for goodness' sake, Stuart, calm down!' Her face tightened with exasperation. 'What a fuss about nothing! They paid, and they paid well. And if it comes to that,

I've put at least as much hard graft into Anything Goes as you, and as much money——'

She stopped abruptly, conscious of Debbie, who was sitting at her untidy desk, avidly lapping up every word. Stuart shot her a hostile look and she sighed inwardly. Too often lately, she reflected, since they had somehow drifted into a closer personal relationship, he had acted the part of the lordly proprietor, trying to cast her in the role of a marginally superior Debbie. She walked past him and, dropping her bag on the desk, began leafing mechanically through the morning's mail. It was almost as though he resented the fact that, pound for pound, hour for hour, she put in as much as he did. But if one day they were going to marry, what did it matter anyway?

Engrossed in her own thoughts, she hardly registered at first what he was saying, but then she looked up sharply.

'Go to the Birthday Lunch? What on earth are you talking about, Stu?'

He grinned at her, his bad temper forgotten, and flourished some embossed cards in front of her. 'What I say. I've just managed to wangle us both invites to the Lunch—and don't ask me how. It's a favour for a favour.' He gave her a knowing look.

Charlotte gazed at him, her grey eyes widening in horror as she finally registered what he was saying. 'B-but that's impossible. We can't!'

'Rubbish—and don't be a fool, of course we can.' His eyes travelled down her slim body and he frowned. 'It's just a pity that you can't go home and change, but there isn't time.'

'No!' Charlotte spoke more loudly than she had intended. 'I-I mean, I'm not going.' She put down several letters on the desk. 'File these, will you please, Debbie. I'll deal with them on Monday. Then you can go.' She spoke calmly enough, but beneath the tranquil surface her mind was seething with apprehension.

They waited in silence until the girl had gone, then Stuart swung round on her, his face flushed with anger. 'Now look, you little fool, I had to practically eat dirt to get my hands on these tickets. Can't you see what a great chance this is? We're new in business here and we need to see and be seen. Actors, local nobs, embassy bigwigs, they'll all be there, and before the Lunch is over I want as many of them as possible to register two little words—Anything Goes.'

Charlotte stared at him mutely for a moment. Yes, of course, Stu was right—they must go. It was an opportunity they could not afford to miss. And besides, she reasoned with herself, there would be hordes there; she would surely be able to keep her distance from—from anyone she would rather not meet. No doubt she would just be able to sit quietly, leaving the easy-tongued Stuart to do all the talking, then afterwards slide away in the crowd, without any sort of confrontation.

'All right, I'll go. Just give me five minutes to spruce myself up.'

He leaned against the desk, watching her complacently. 'And mind you put up your hair.' He was almost jovial, now that he had won his point. 'You know I don't like it dangling all round your face. It looks so untidy.'

'Very good, sir.'

Charlotte smiled at him over her shoulder, but when she had shut herself into the dark, airless little box that masqueraded as a cloakroom, the smile faded and she stared into the small mirror at her sombre reflection.

What in the world had she done, she asked herself, not for the first time, allowing herself to become emotionally as well as professionally entangled with Stuart Fletcher? And yet at first it had seemed sensible, even desirable. Even though he was, at twenty-six, only one year older than she was, he had so much more business acumen—take this matter of the Lunch—and linking their out-of-office lives had appeared just as sensible. Charlotte sighed at her solemn-eyed self, then hearing Stuart impatiently banging around at the filing cabinet, she reapplied a hasty coat of soft pink lip-gloss to her wide, almost over-wide mouth and lightly powdered her nose.

Her hair lay on her shoulders in heavy, dark russet strands. Usually she only wore it down like this at home, but this morning she had overslept and had only had time to comb it through quickly. Now she dragged it into a fat ponytail with a rubber band, then curled it into a loose twist, securing it with a few hairpins which she had in her bag. Mmm, it would just about hold if she was lucky. She studied her reflection again. Yes, Stuart was right. With her hair down, in riotous confusion, she looked too young, hardly more than seventeen, but now she had achieved the sleeker, more finished look of a would-be successful businesswoman.

She went out, smoothing the unpressed pleats of her soft grey flannel skirt and tucking the neat white blouse more securely into her waistband.

'That's better.'

Stuart, who was brushing imaginary fair hairs from his immaculate London-styled suit, smiled at her approvingly and she smiled back at him. After all, it *was* the good of the business he was thinking of, and besides, he was very handsome.

'Keep still a minute.' He did up the very top pearl button on her blouse, then helped her into the matching grey flannel jacket. 'As I said, a pity there wasn't time for you to change, but this is your working uniform, after all.'

He smoothed down his carefully knotted silk tie, switched on the answering machine and ushered her out.

They were late, in spite of Stuart's impatient haste, and when they reached the marquee beside the River Avon most of the guests were already seated and Charlotte, her cheeks burning, was glad to drop into her place, to concentrate on eating and making polite small talk with the man beside her, leaving Stuart to entertain their near neighbours rather more enthusiastically.

But in spite of herself, her eyes strayed frequently towards the narrow gap between the crowded tables, through which she had a diagonal, almost profile view of Jude Renton. Even when she determinedly did not look, awareness of his presence was in every pore of her body and, through the subdued noises of twenty conversations, as she smiled yet again at the man beside her or replied to one of Stuart's quips, she could hear that familiar, ringing, confident laugh.

When the speeches and toasts '...to the immortal memory...' were finally ended, she retrieved her grey leather handbag and stood up, keeping herself screened from Jude by a large group of guests who seemed to be in no hurry to leave. Her one desire now was to escape from the marquee unseen, but Stuart had other ideas, and when she put her hand on his arm he shook it off.

'Where do you think you're going? We're not leaving yet.'

There was a slight note of belligerence in his voice, and Charlotte looked at him, her heart sinking. He had drunk his way fairly steadily through the meal and now his face was flushed, his eyes very bright.

'We're not leaving yet. We're going to do some circulating—there's plenty of useful contacts among this lot. For instance——' He called across to a young man in a lounge suit, 'Hey there, Brian!'

As he came up to them, Charlotte recognised the reporter from a local radio station, who had, after much prompting from Stuart, and quite a few late evening sessions in local pubs, done a small feature on them. She stood, a polite smile fixed into place, as the two men exchanged back-slapping pleasantries. Her head was beginning to throb tightly, from the close heat in the marquee and the unaccustomed alcohol, while her shoes, after a morning spent pounding the Stratford pavements, felt several sizes too small. She closed her eyes for a moment. As soon as she got back to her flat she would kick them off and collapse on the sofa with a pot of tea. Marvellous!

'Hello, Mr Renton. I'm Brian Rollins from Arden Radio.'

Charlotte started convulsively. Her eyes flew wide open, but somehow—somehow, she steeled herself not to turn. Jude was standing right behind her. She could smell the faint tang of his expensive aftershave, the heavier aroma of his cigar, and yet it was neither of these but that much more subtle sixth sense which she had always had where he was concerned which now made the hair on her neck prickle, her pulses race, at the certainty that if she stepped back one pace, she would feel that hard, strong body.

She became dimly aware that Stuart was moving smoothly into action, introducing himself, his whole bearing assuming that familiar combination of boyish good humour and suave man of the business world, which she sometimes guiltily felt sure he practised each morning in the mirror. She herself felt as though every muscle was tensed ready for flight, while her busy fingers plucked at the heavy gilt buckle on her bag. She heard Jude's voice, cool, perfectly polite—only she was aware of his desire, too, for escape, and a frisson of irritation, at being trapped, that only she caught.

'Hey, Jude—you don't mind if I call you Jude? I've just remembered.' Brian Rollins' hand was gripping her arm. 'This young lady is from round here as well. Local girl, local boy make good. Maybe I could do something on it.' The pressure from his hand was inexorable, yet somehow Charlotte was turning in slow motion. 'She's come back to Stratford to run a new tourist venture with Stuart here, and they're doing very nicely.'

Charlotte slowly raised her eyes to meet Jude's dark blue ones, cold and inscrutable, but with no hint of surprise; he had no doubt recognised her earlier, but like her had sought to avoid a meeting. At last, very deliberately, he spoke, without looking at either of the men, keeping his eyes unwaveringly on her.

'We have met. In fact, we're very old friends, aren't we, Charlotte?'

His voice was perfectly smooth and expressionless; the unsmiling mockery patent in his eyes was for her alone. It seemed to her that in the rest of the marquee the lights were dimming, everyone else slipping away into darkness, while Jude held her, held them both, in a merciless spotlight. Her own pulsebeat was pounding in her ears . . . She struggled for composure. She could not stand for ever staring wide-eyed at him, not with the two men beside them straining almost visibly to catch every delicate nuance of what was being said. Somehow, pride came to her rescue.

'We certainly are.' She smiled up at him, tilting her chin at a defiant angle. 'Hello, Jude, long time no see.'

She had managed to make her tone deliberately light, and his fine, dark brows drew down in a frown.

'I didn't——' Stuart began, but Jude cut through his words, his eyes still locked with hers.

'Yes, it is a long time. Seven years, to be exact. You've changed.' His glance swept down her body, taking in every detail of her deceptively simple suit, her dove-grey kid leather shoes and bag, then returned to her face. 'I didn't know you were back in Stratford.'

'Well, it's hardly front page news in the *Stratford Herald* if *I* come back.'

Charlotte tried to smile faintly, then Stuart was at her side, his hand on her arm. Why must everyone keep clutching her in that proprietorial way? She tried to withdraw slightly, but he held on to her tightly.

'Charlotte returned with me.' His voice was over-loud, as though uneasily he sensed the tensions between the other two and wanted to break in. 'We worked together in London and now we've opened up our own business in the sticks—first of many, I hope. We're a good team. Well, I believe in husband and wife working together— the secret of many a successful showbiz marriage, I'm sure you'll agree, Renton?'

She saw anger quicken in Jude's eyes. 'Husband and wife?' He favoured Stuart with one swift, annihilating glance, then turned back to Charlotte, who was beginning to feel as though she had stepped out into a minefield which was now threatening to explode around her at any second.

'No,' she said emphatically. 'I-I mean, no, we're not married. Although,' she added hurriedly, as she saw Stuart's face, 'we *are* unofficially engaged.'

She felt not only tired but suddenly overwhelmingly dispirited, the result no doubt of alcohol at lunch time— it did not agree with her and she never drank if she could avoid it. And besides, it was clear that the two men had taken an immediate and violent dislike to each other, leaving the sharp-eyed Brian Rollins as an interested spectator. Stuart seemed to have forgotten all his intentions of building up useful contacts and was scowling openly up at Jude, while Jude, she was exasperated to see, was wearing his most bland and therefore most irritating expression. He removed his cigar and looked at it with an expression of intense disfavour, then tossed it down and ground it out under his heel.

Charlotte felt a spiral of anger mounting rapidly inside her. She hitched up her bag squarely on to her shoulder and held out her hand.

'Goodbye, Brian. Nice to meet you again.' She smiled at him. 'Do drop into the office any time you're passing—we've got some really great ideas on the boil.'

She inclined her head coolly to the man standing in front of her. 'See you around, Jude.'

He did not acknowledge her, but as she walked off, leaving Stuart no alternative but to follow, she knew that his eyes were still on her.

CHAPTER TWO

CHARLOTTE was already hurrying along Waterside when Stuart caught up with her.

'You realise you made me look an absolute fool back there?'

'What?' She stared at him in amazement. 'What on earth do you mean, Stu?'

'You didn't tell me you know Jude Renton.'

'Oh, didn't I?' There was the faintest hint of warning in her voice, which he seemed quite oblivious to.

'No, you didn't. And why the hell not?'

'Oh, I'm sorry.' Still raw from the encounter with the man himself, she was in no mood now for another bout of Stuart's bad humour. 'I didn't realise you wanted a blow-by-blow account of my early life,' she snapped, but then caught herself up short. Don't let Jude do it, she thought fiercely, don't let him have the tiniest influence on you.

She slipped her arm through his. 'I suppose I didn't think it was that important.'

'Not that important!' He stood stock still on the pavement. 'Listen, Charlotte.' He shook her arm emphatically. 'Contacts—that's what counts. In this business, like any other, it's who you know, who can pull strings for you, that matters. How can you be so naïve?'

Charlotte, tight-lipped, pulled her arm away and walked off down the street so quickly that he only caught up with her on the doorstep of the small terraced house where she rented the ground-floor flat.

'Really, Charlotte, I don't know what's got into you!' When she ignored him and went on fumbling in her bag for her key, he said, 'Jude Renton's one of the hottest names in show business and you know him. Well, make use of that knowledge, will you? I can quite see why you wouldn't want to. He's an arrogant bastard—all but ignored me—but we can still make use of him.'

Stu, trying to make use of Jude Renton? Charlotte almost laughed out loud at the appalling picture—a fleecy lamb sizing up to a tiger; yes, that analogy was fairly apt, she decided. But then the thought of her being forced into any more contact with Jude made her recoil violently.

'Now listen, Stuart,' she said urgently, 'whatever ideas you've got about Jude, forget them. Don't tangle with him. You'll regret it, I promise you. And now,' she pushed open the blue-painted front door, 'I must go.' Then as he made to follow her inside, 'No, I'd rather you didn't come in. I've got some more reading up to do for that witchcraft tour next week.'

She smiled at him and, to atone for her earlier snappiness, willed herself not to turn away from his kiss. She closed the front door and leaned against it for a moment. Well, at least Stu only seemed to be concerned with her abject failure to capitalise on her unsuspected acquaintance with Jude. There had not been the faintest twinge of jealousy in his reaction or awareness of her own inner turmoil, she thought, and she did not know whether to be glad or sorry.

As she slowly straightened up, she caught her reflection in the hall mirror and stared contemplatively at herself. She was very pale. It must be from the shock of

coming face to face with Jude again without warning.
Jude. Her mouth twisted suddenly and she watched with
almost clinical detachment as tears sprang to her eyes,
blurring her image.

'... You didn't tell me you knew Jude Renton...'

Well, what should I have told you? That I loved him,
and he broke my heart when I was hardly eighteen?

Now, there was just one tiny thing to be grateful for.
That first appalling moment was over. She had faced
squarely Jude's cold hostility towards her, and surely it
could never be as bad again? If they ever happened to
come face to face in future, they would be able somehow
to concoct a few minutes' brittle small talk, so that those
around them would be quite unaware of the shadow
which hung over—or rather between them—for ever.

'Go on out into the garden, love, you look really tired.
I'll make a nice cup of tea.'

'Oh, I'm fine, Gran, honestly.'

Charlotte smiled reassuringly at her grandmother, but
none the less, once outside she was glad to sink into one
of the faded canvas chairs. The garden was small, like
the house, which was the nineteenth-century lodge
cottage to the Manor House, and was enclosed by high
hedges, so that even in winter it was sometimes snug
enough to sit out of doors. This afternoon, the spring
sunshine had all the illusion of summer warmth and the
sweet, honeyed smell from clumps of white jonquils
drifted up to her.

She leaned back, her closed eyelids golden against the
sun. She had not intended coming until the following
day for her usual Sunday tea-time visit, but in spite of
her earlier longing for a solitary afternoon, some inner
restlessness, a hardly conscious need for comfort and

reassurance, had brought her back to her childhood home.

Her father had died when she was a child and her mother had been forced to give up the rented house in the next village and move back here with her mother-in-law. When she remarried a few years later and moved to Nottingham, Charlotte, fighting against another upheaval in her short life, had clung tenaciously to her grandmother. Looking back, the older Charlotte realised wryly that her mother had relinquished her child almost too easily to the glowing prospect of another marriage, but somehow it had never mattered, for she had found here all the loving stability she would ever need.

As she sipped her tea, she described the celebrations and how the posies had been such a great success. She hesitated, but it was no use; her grandmother would be sure to find out sooner or later.

'Oh, and by the way,' she said casually, 'we went to the Birthday Lunch.'

'Oh, yes, and how did you manage that?'

'Well, actually, Stu managed to get us invitations,' Charlotte said reluctantly.

'Mmm.' Her grandmother's placid, rosy face assumed its usual disapproving expression whenever Stuart's name came up in conversation, which was as seldom as Charlotte could manage. 'Trust that young man!'

Charlotte opened her mouth to protest, then closed it resignedly. What was the point? From the first time she had brought Stu here, the old lady had made it abundantly apparent that she did not like him, and nothing—his smiling good humour, his smart yet conservative suits, the regular bouquets—had sweetened her one jot.

'Did you see anyone you know?'

'Y-yes, Gran.' She swallowed. 'That is, I saw Jude.'

'I rather thought you might have done.' Her grand-mother's voice was dry and she began stacking the cups on the tray with unnecessary vigour. 'Now you sit there. You look proper done in, my girl. Been burning the candle at both ends, I don't doubt.'

But when she had gone, Charlotte sprang to her feet, the same restlessness that had brought her here now driving her to—to do what? She roamed round the garden, then under a low archway to the tiny vegetable plot with its neat rows of early lettuce and spring onions. This garden too was enclosed by another, taller hedge of copper beech, and beyond it she glimpsed the topmost branches of the huge old walnut tree in the Manor grounds. At the sight of it, a faint, sad smile twisted her mouth, then on a sudden impulse she darted over to the small shed in the corner and peered behind it. Yes, the hole in the beech hedge was still there, although surely much smaller than she remembered? But no one except herself, Jude and Simon had ever used it, so no doubt it had become overgrown since that long-dead time when she had pushed through it half a dozen times every day with such ease.

She was still very slim, though—some people even thought her fragile until they discovered otherwise—and, drawn by a magnetic force that she could not resist, but which, she realised now, had been building insidiously inside her since that first moment when she saw Jude again, she scrambled her way through, to stand in the unkempt grass on the far side, brushing away some dead leaves which clung to her aquamarine velour tracksuit.

Just for a moment, long-buried, half-exultant, half-apprehensive emotions churned inside her, as though she were that child again and waiting, breath suspended, for the unknown. But then other memories, which over and over again she had thrust from her and which she thought she had erased for ever, flooded in, obliterating everything.

...a skinny little girl, russet hair in two fat plaits... 'Wait for me, Si'... 'Oh, go away, Charley, or I'll pull your hair—you're just a stupid girl'... 'Please, Jude, Si says I can't come fishing with you—*please* let me come! I promise I won't talk this time, and I won't cry when you catch a fish'... 'Come on then, but no yattering, or off you go... I said yes, Si, she *can* come'...

The young leaves on the walnut tree rippled silver against the keen edge of the wind, and as Charlotte shivered, thrusting her hands into her pouch pockets, she saw, disbelievingly, that a child's swing still hung from the lowest branch. After her accident, the twins' father had threatened to remove it, but somehow he never had—and here it still was. She walked slowly across and sat down cautiously on the wooden seat, her arms hooked around the ropes, letting it take her idly back and forth.

...'Push me, Jude. I want to go right up as far as the sky'... 'No, you're high enough already, Charley'... 'I'll push you, Charley. Is that high enough—high enough—high enough?'... The world spinning, gyrating sickeningly... Jude snatching her up from the ground and walking—no, running to the house with her, his mouth set and fierce... looking down at her, his face whirling, receding at a terrifying rate... 'Don't tell on Si, Charley. Whatever you do, don't tell...' So, of course, she hadn't—not even when old Doctor Sutton had looked at her with patent disbelief but had kept his own counsel—and Si had been kind to her for at least a week ... Jude and Si, Jude and Si and Charley, Jude and Charley...

She stood up abruptly and, hunched against the chill wind, walked among the gnarled old fruit trees into the Manor gardens. They were almost as uncared for as the orchard, and she felt a deep sadness. Poor Mrs Renton— she had loved the gardens almost as much as the Manor itself and yet, after Simon's death, she had been quite unable to stay here, so Mr Renton had been forced to take her to live in Jersey and to lease the lovely old house—first to a girls' school, then to a health farm, both of which had folded. The lease was now being advertised again and Charlotte wondered what hopeful enterprise might take it over next—perhaps the acolytes of some Eastern guru would soon take the place of the flabby businessmen who had so entertained the locals as they pounded with set faces round the nearby lanes.

Weeds grew up among the paving stones of the terrace and her footsteps, even in trainers, made a forlorn, hollow echo against the walls. This was Mr Renton's billiard room, but had once been the library, and when she peered through the dirty sash window, she could see the empty mahogany bookshelves which lined the walls still.

Here were the french doors, leading to the ballroom. Charlotte pressed her face against one of them and it moved slightly, so that she realised that it was only held on the catch. When she got home, she would give the agent a ring—anyone could get in and do all sorts of damage. Hesitantly, her heart beating fast, she put out her hand to slowly open the door and slipped inside, the chandeliers above her head rustling softly in the sudden draught.

She dropped down, rather shakily, on to one of the window seats as a spasm of raw emotion seized her. Seven years. It was seven years since that final, fatal party in this room, the evening which had splintered their relationship for ever...a relationship which had begun almost from the time Charlotte could walk, when, deprived of children—girls—of her own age, she had tagged on behind the twins, six years older, with a grim determination not to be left behind. Momentarily, she felt again a shadow of that pain which had gripped her every time the boys had gone away, first to boarding school, then to drama college, leaving her feeling bereft overnight of a vital part of her own self.

Just for one second she allowed herself to relive the joy she had felt when Mrs Renton told her that they had both been offered a season at Stratford. It had been almost too much to bear, though it had proved evanescent enough, for from the beginning, the seventeen-year-old Charlotte had understood, with a mature wisdom which she had not known until then she possessed, that the relationship was altered irrevocably.

That first day, wandering restlessly in the cottage garden, where she was supposedly weeding, she had heard cars arriving, doors slamming, and, unable to stop herself, even while she was frightened by her own temerity, she had pushed through the hedge, run across the orchard and out on to the terrace.

There were a crowd of young people, milling exuberantly about Mr and Mrs Renton. She saw Jude, of course, caught the flicker of amused irritation on his face, and shrank back, brushing her grubby hands down her faded dungarees, but too late for escape, as kind Mrs Renton spotted her and determinedly drew her, scarlet-faced, into the group. Then Jude's voice was in her ear. 'Still the tomboy, I see! For God's sake, Charley, why didn't you put some decent clothes on?' He grinned at her, only half joking, and gave her a casual hug, before abandoning her, almost as though for deliberate contrast, to two well-scrubbed young women in pretty Laura Ashley smocks. Somehow, Charlotte had refused a drink and escaped, to wander forlornly all afternoon in the Manor grounds, and by the time she went home for tea she had gained a dry-eyed composure that would have fooled anyone who did not look too closely.

She had seen the twins occasionally during that season, and twice just managed to avoid bumping into Jude as she ran for her bus, in her despised school uniform. One day, their mother had passed on his message that if she wanted to come in to see a preview . . . but she had smilingly refused.

All at once, Charlotte sprang up from the window seat, to pace the echoing length of the ballroom. She should never have come back here, never have pushed through the hedge this final time. Too late, she knew that, but she knew also that she could not leave yet—something was tugging at her, detaining her against her will, so that she must go on and relive those last few searing events, when her whole world had seemed to slam brutally to a halt, and then slowly shatter into fragments around her . . .

When the invitation to the end-of-season party, which the Rentons were giving for the company, had come, her first blind instinct had been to refuse. But Mrs Renton had written over the top, 'I do so hope you can come, Charley', so she had quickly written her acceptance, then dropped it just as quickly into the postbox at the lodge gates.

Then, that late afternoon, just days before the party, she had slipped through the hedge again—and surely it already seemed to have shrunk since the last time, only going then because she was sure that everyone was out and she was quite safe. She had roamed through the grounds, then into the huge conservatory, where she closed the door behind her and felt the perfumed warmth spring up around her.

She had been right at the far end, trapped, when she heard the door open softly and through the tangled branches of a jasmine saw Jude. A strange wave of shame and aversion—not to him but to the idea of his finding her there—flooded through her, but even as she tensed to duck under an old garden hammock, she heard his voice.

'It's no use hiding, Charley. I saw you from the house, so come on out!'

Charlotte straightened up, hot with foolishness, though at the same time intensely grateful that today she was dressed, not in jeans, but in her best white angora sweater and the short grey skirt which showed off her long, slim legs.

'H-hello, Jude,' was all she could breathlessly manage, as he sauntered up to her. He leaned against the staging, his arms folded, his dark blue eyes almost jet against the light. He seemed much older than when she had last seen him; the boyish features had at last vanished, to be replaced by a face which, though even more strikingly handsome, already bore the hard, strong lines of a man, a man who knew not only what he wanted but that he would achieve it.

'Where have you been hiding yourself, Charley? You haven't been avoiding us, have you? And you've changed. No tomboy any more—quite the beautiful young woman.'

His eyes were intent on her, and, suddenly ill at ease with him in a totally new kind of way, she began plucking at a glossy leaf beside her.

'W-where's Simon?' she asked.

Jude shrugged, then pulled a rueful face. 'Running through one of his scenes yet again, that he just can't get right.' His voice sounded almost angry for a moment, then he sighed and all at once, with no warning, pulled her into his arms, his head against her hair. As she tensed, he went on, 'Oh God, Charley, what shall I do? I've tried to help him, but he just blows his top and pushes me away.'

There was no anger now, only a ragged hurt of the one twin for the other, and she put her arms round him, aching to comfort him. After a few moments, he drew back his head, and in the fading greenish light, his eyes darkened to a sapphire black.

'Oh, my little Charley!' His voice was unsteady and he lifted a tendril of her hair to his lips, then just as gently bent his head and kissed her mouth, as his hands slipped inside her sweater to hold her close against his body.

At first, that had seemed enough, but when he held her from him to look into her eyes again, and she smiled up at him, shyly aware of the yearning that must be revealed in them, Jude caught her to him, roughly this time, and they clung together as they slipped to their knees, on to the old mattress from the garden hammock...

Then, afterwards, Jude, his face still flushed from passion, looking at her, guilty and appalled. 'Oh God, I'm sorry, Charley. Why—why didn't you stop me?'

But why should she have? Why—when she loved him more than any other being in the universe? Avoiding each other's eyes, they had got dressed, she dragging on her clothes with shaking fingers, and she had pushed past him, wanting only to be alone, with her rapture and her anguish.

And then, a few nights later, the party... Her hair up, dressed in a new soft blue-green smock dress that Gran had made for her, she had walked round to the main drive, past the rhododendrons and gloomy Victorian conifers. Charlotte knew she was early, but her trembling impatience to see Jude again had driven her to come, overcoming her shyness and making her totally indifferent to the fact that she would almost certainly be the first arrival.

On the terrace she had paused, as she heard through the open billiard room window Simon's voice, raised angrily. She had turned, unwilling to eavesdrop on the brothers, but when Jude began to speak, she stopped dead.

'But Si,' his voice was level, though obviously controlled by a supreme effort, 'it's the opportunity of a lifetime. I have to go, you know I do.'

Charlotte risked a sidelong glance into the room and saw them facing each other across the green baize table—Jude gripping its edge, Simon glaring at him, a half empty glass in his hand.

'I suppose you agree with what they're all saying—oh, don't think I haven't heard,' as Jude tried to break in, 'Jude Renton acting at half-cock, so he doesn't show his brother up too much.'

A terrible, sick feeling was washing through her. Poor Si—and poor Jude! She leaned back against the wall and closed her eyes against the stab of pity for them both, then went very still, as she heard Simon again.

'And what about Charley?'

'What about her?' Jude's voice was suddenly glacial and she was glad she could not see his face.

'Well, you know she's crazy about you. Doesn't that matter?'

Charlotte heard no more. Her hands to her ears, she rushed headlong across the terrace and hid herself in the walled garden until it was safe to emerge among a group of guests.

Simon, drinking his way relentlessly through the evening...Jude, cold and reserved, as though deliberately distancing himself from her and that magical moment among the scented jasmine and stephanotis; even calling on another young actor to dance with her when, drawn like a timid, fragile moth to a flame, she had at last gone close to him...that roll of drums when Jude, unsmiling and hurried, as though he had no taste for it, had announced that he had been offered a part in Bellini's latest film and was leaving for Italy the next day...

She had turned her eyes from Jude to Simon's poor, hurt face, and escaped to the solitude of the garden, where Simon followed her and abruptly asked her to marry him. 'You love him, and I love him. So——' his face twisted '—we'll cheer each other up.'

And because, physically at least, he was so like his brother, and she had felt, in that moment of bleak, dead despair, that if she could not have one she could at least have the other, Charlotte had weakly accepted. Nevertheless, taken completely unaware, she had needed at least as much acting ability as Jude possessed when Simon, jubilantly triumphant, had proclaimed, 'And now Charley and I have something to tell you all, as well.'

When the congratulating throng had eased, Jude had come to her. He took her hand. 'Are you sure—quite sure, Charley?'

With a tremendous effort she had met his troubled gaze. 'Of course, Jude. Quite sure.'

She saw the relief in his eyes, and that hurt her more than anything, but somehow, as Jude, his lips chill, gave her a formal kiss, she kept her smile intact.

'Be happy, Charlotte.' . . .

In the gallery above the ballroom, a floorboard creaked softly and she came out of her anguished reverie with a sharp jolt of fear. But then she smiled ruefully. The old house was playing tricks on her—that had sounded almost like a footfall. Still, it was time to go.

She took a few steps towards the french doors, then stood as though frozen in stillness, her hand to her throat, as someone—a man—came out of the shadows and unhurriedly descended the wide staircase.

Jude paused on the bottom step and they stared at one another.

'You're very pale, Charlotte.' His face was an unsmiling mask. 'What's the matter—been seeing ghosts?'

CHAPTER THREE

AT LEAST Jude had made no attempt to detain her or even to pursue her. For days, Charlotte clung to this single consoling thought, as for the hundredth time her mind went back to that appalling moment. With the myriad emotions those scourging memories had aroused in her, her one instinct on seeing Jude had been to turn and flee headlong from the ballroom and across the orchard to the sanctuary of her grandmother's garden.

As she left her car, she felt the first threatening spot of rain on her face and saw the lowering clouds building above her. She pulled a rueful face. The fine weather of the Birthday celebrations three days before had well and truly disappeared and now here she was, on this bleak Cotswold hillside, exposed to anything the elements might throw at her.

She huddled further into her heavy yellow PVC cagoule and stood uncertainly, looking around her. Where should she go first? To the enclosure which held the Rollright Stones themselves, the so-called King's Men, the circle of weathered Neolithic stones, centre of so many superstitious tales and whispered fears and which, she hoped, would keep Professor Kameyama happy when she brought him here in a few days' time? Or across a windswept, muddy field to the Whispering Knights? Perhaps the rain would hold off a little longer, so, leaving the circle until later, she made off in the direction of the Knights, her wellington boots squelching loudly.

By the time she reached the cluster of stones, though, the rain was pelting down, the heavy drops splattering on her guide book as she tried vainly to shelter against the hedge. But then she went across to the stones and laid her ear gingerly to the crevice where, local legend had it, could still be heard the whisperings as the knights plotted against their king...

Surely that was a faint sound, almost a murmur? Charlotte jerked back, then gave a shamefaced smile. How stupid! It had only been the wind. This place and all its stories of witchcraft and strange sinister happenings—not all of which were in the safely distant past—must be getting to her. The Stones were not malign, living creatures plotting evil against her, they were nothing more than misshapen lumps of grey limestone. But even so, she hurried back up the field without a single backward glance.

Once safely on the road, she glanced at her watch. Time for a quick look at the circle, then back to Stratford in good time for her dinner date with Stuart. But first a leisurely bath, to soak the enormous blister which she could feel on her ankle, from the chafing of her brand new yellow wellingtons.

From the circle, she limped painfully towards where her car was parked, but then stood, bewildered. No blue Mini, or any other vehicle, was now parked in the muddy layby. Her car had gone. Too late, calling herself all kinds of fool, she remembered that out here, with no one else around, it had not seemed necessary to lock the doors.

She stood for a few moments miserably chewing her lip, as she fought the desire to crumple up in a pool of tears. But tears would not help on this rainy, deserted road—only she could help herself. She must walk back to the main road, try to hitch a lift, at any rate get to a phone. Yes, that was it—she would ring the police, and then Stuart, who would have to come and fetch her. She groaned inwardly at what he would have to say about the unlocked doors, then shouldered her bag and set off.

Nothing passed her in the lane, and when she finally hobbled to the main Stratford to Oxford road, every one of the few cars had, of course, lone male drivers, all no doubt perfectly harmless, but none the less...

Thank heavens she had at least taken her bag with her, otherwise she would have been forced to change all the locks at her flat... Lost in her thoughts, she was scarcely aware of the dark blue low-slung Jaguar which passed her, travelling very fast towards Oxford. She came to as the driver braked hard, tyres screaming on the wet road, and when she turned she saw, with a flicker of uneasiness, that the man—she could see his outline half turned towards her—was reversing almost as fast.

She looked around her anxiously, but the road was deserted in both directions. All the unpleasant stories she had ever heard leaped into her mind, welding together into a tight lump of solid fear. As she turned away again, she heard the car door open and at the sound of footsteps crunching on the road, she quickened her own pace. Perhaps she would be able to reach the village at the foot of the hill and——

A hand caught her roughly by the arm. With a gasp of sick terror, she whirled round and saw—Jude Renton. Jude? But it simply couldn't be—not out of all the people in the world that it could be. Stupidly, she stared up into his angry eyes as the rain poured down both their faces.

'For God's sake, Charlotte,' he gave her arm an impatient shake, 'stop playing stupid games! Didn't you hear me calling you?'

'N-no, I didn't.'

She had been incapable of hearing anything above the thunderous beat of her own heart, and even now its rhythm was refusing to steady. Rather the contrary.

'What the hell are you——?'

He broke off as a stinging gust of rain lashed them, then, settling his grip more firmly on her elbow, he half dragged her back to his car and opened the passenger door.

'Get in!' He was shouting against the wind.

Charlotte hung back. The rain, the wind, a long, painful walk now seemed suddenly a small price to pay and infinitely preferable——

She just had time for, 'No, I'd rather not——' when Jude swung her up into his arms and dumped her, with as much finesse as if he were humping a sack of potatoes, down on to the seat. He slammed the door and threw himself in beside her. He leaned forward and switched off the cassette that was softly playing an Elton John tape, then sat back in his seat, regarding her for a few moments in silence, his blue-black eyes gleaming with some vivid emotion which she did not quite like.

'And now perhaps you'll tell me what you're up to. Presumably,' his eyes flicked over her, 'even in that outfit, you're not off to man the lifeboats?'

She ignored the sarcasm. 'I've been to the Rollrights,' she said tightly, 'and when I got back, my car had been stolen. I—I forgot to lock it.'

'Still the same casual Charlotte, I see.'

His lips twisted momentarily and the nebulous unease at being alone with him, trapped in his car, crystallised into something very like panic. Somehow, she must get away.

'Thank you for letting me warm up a bit. I'll be all right now.'

She took a firm grip on the door handle, but as she turned it Jude leaned across her and seized her wrist.

'Look, I have to get back to Stratford.' The fear, and the unwelcome sensation of his warm hand on her, sharpened her voice. 'You're going the wrong way, so please let me get out. Unless—— ' she hesitated as another gust of wind rocked the car '—you could possibly give me a lift to Chipping Norton. It's only just off the road and I can get to a phone there, and—and ask Stuart to come and fetch me.' Then, when he did not reply, she wound up, 'I'd be most grateful.'

She sensed a release of tension in him and he slackened his grip. 'Of course I'll give you a lift, Charlotte, if you want one. You know you only have to ask.'

His voice was smooth, though there was an undercurrent to it that disturbed her, and when she looked round at him she somehow felt certain that beneath the bland, inscrutable smile, mockery lurked.

Jude paused, his hand on her seat-belt. 'Don't you want to take that thing off?' He gestured derisively towards the unyielding yellow straitjacket. 'You'll be more comfortable without it.'

'Oh, no,' she said hastily. Somehow, as long as she was cocooned in its folds, it was giving her silent reassurance that her enforced stay in Jude's car was to be a transitory one, minutes only. 'I'd have to get out to pull it off. It's not worth it just for a few miles.'

He shrugged acquiescence, then fastened their seat-belts and switched on the powerful engine. Charlotte leaned back into the luxurious upholstery, and only as she relaxed marginally did she realise how taut she had been since the moment Jude had appeared on the scene, like an apparition summoned up by the witch of Rollright, and far more disturbing even than the loss of her car. But she still could not relax her guard. It was just as well it was only a brief distance, and the speed which they were doing meant that it would be a short if not exactly sweet journey. Perhaps he was as anxious as she to pull into the square at Chipping Norton and decant his unwilling passenger.

She stretched out her tired legs, then winced as she bumped her sore heel.

'What's the matter?' He glanced at her.

'Oh, it's these new wellingtons. I think I've got a blister.'

'Take them off.'

'I told you—it's not worth it. And besides, I don't fancy having to put them back on again in a couple of minutes.'

'Suit yourself.' Jude's voice was laconic, and he returned his attention to the road.

By turning her head slightly, Charlotte could study his lean, almost sharp profile in perfect safety... The dark hair across the brow, the straight Grecian nose, fine eyebrows above those intense blue eyes—a face saved from the too-regular hardness of perfect beauty by the long sweep of dark lashes—too long by half for a boy, her grandmother had always teased him—and that curving, sensual mouth, which now, she realised with a jolt, had a small, secret smile playing around it. He must be aware of her eyes on him. Scarlet-faced and furious with herself, she turned away to look out of her window, then started in horror.

'Hey! We're way past the turn.'

'That's right.' He shot her a glance in which the smile was quite open and that frisson of unease hardened into anger.

'Now look, Jude, I don't know what you think you're up to—but just you turn round and take me——'

'Sorry, but I'm in a hurry.'

She stared at him, seeing the gleam of white teeth, and her lips tightened in mingled exasperation, apprehension, and a frustrated sense of her own utter helplessness.

'But you promised.' She only just managed to keep the quiver out of her voice. 'You said you'd give me a lift to Chipping Norton.'

'Uh-uh.' Jude's voice was a purr of malevolent satisfaction. '*You* said I'd give you a lift to Chipping Norton—*I* said I'll give you a lift.'

'Well, it's the same thing.' Momentarily, the exasperation won, so that she almost snarled. 'I—I have to get back home as soon as I can.' She considered, briefly, explaining that she had a date with Stuart, but somehow she felt sure that this would hardly be likely to entice Jude to co-operate. Instead, she decided on another ploy. 'Surely even you can see that I've got to inform the police, so I absolutely demand that you——'

'Oh, shut up, Charlotte!' Jude's voice was all at once rasping with anger. 'And don't be a shrew. I've been dealing with one of those all day in the rehearsal room, and I've had enough. So, if you know what's good for you, you'll sit still and stop trying to rile me, or you might just succeed, and then we'll both regret it.'

The warning menace of his tone and in the look he flashed her was all too clear. Charlotte, frightened into silence, set her teeth on her intended retort and contented herself with tapping one muddy foot against the pale blue carpet and staring mutinously out of the window. Behind her impassive face, though, her mind spun in tumult. What did he intend to do with her, for heaven's sake? Take her with him, presumably, to wherever he was going—Oxford, almost certainly. And when they arrived, what then?

She surveyed herself without enthusiasm. Wellingtons, old jeans, cagoule—her gear was hardly town wear. Oh well, perhaps finally, after all this cat-and-mousing with her, Jude would give her a lift back to Stratford. He would have to be back for the evening performance and so, with luck, *she* could still be in time for her date. Meanwhile, she would have to accept the situation with as good a grace as she could muster, even though her insides were fizzing with the tension of being in this confined space with him, while, with each second of captivity, her nerves were tightening yet another notch.

The spires of the Oxford skyline were approaching at an alarming rate, when Jude slowed at a junction and turned sharp left towards—— Oh God, he wasn't going to Oxford, after all. Of course he wasn't.

'You're going to London.' It was a flat statement, not a question.

'That's right. Where else?'

A quarter of an hour; that was all it would have taken to drop her off, still well within reach of rescue. But no. He was coldly, deliberately following some devious plan of his own, with no thought for her, and she was trapped, trapped with him and the fear that he was engendering in her...

Wait a minute, though. Just ahead there was a huge traffic island. Carefully, Charlotte edged forward, one hand closing on the strap of her bag at her feet, the other easing her seat-belt, and then, as Jude braked sharply, she threw herself sideways, bursting out of the belt and scrabbling at the door handle.

Even in the second that it began to open, though, Jude dragged her back, throwing her against the seat. He slammed the door and accelerated rapidly away as she lay back, overwhelmed by the misery of her failure and a little shaken by her own foolhardiness.

'Don't ever try that bloody fool trick again, do you hear? You could have been killed!'

Jude was very pale, whether from shock or anger she did not know. On balance, the latter, she thought.

'Yes, I hear,' she replied coldly, ostentatiously nursing her right arm, bruised by his grip as he had wrenched her back.

'Once and for all, you're not escaping from me this time, Charlotte.' Jude had recovered his composure and there was a chill hardness in his voice. 'You disappeared at the Lunch and you scuttled from me like a terrified rabbit at the Manor, though you only got away then because I should already have been down at the theatre. Well now, no one—especially that precious little boy-friend of yours——' she winced at his contemptuous tone '—is around to help you, so——' he gave her a mocking smile '—third time lucky. You're staying with me until I choose to release you. I hope that's clear?'

She stared at him. He was doing what he had so often done when they were children, dominating, even frightening her by the magnetism of his powerful personality, and she felt herself slipping helplessly back into that other time. She pulled herself up short. This was utterly ridiculous. She was twenty-five, a grown woman, and here she was, being held against her will, kidnapped in broad daylight. She must fight back somehow, break this insidious spell.

'But you told me that you never wanted to set eyes on me again, remember—seven years ago, at Simon's funeral.'

The word, the name, was out now and she saw, though with no sense of triumph, Jude's mouth tighten involuntarily on a grimace of pain. But when he replied, his voice was perfectly controlled.

'Ah, but you see, I've changed my mind. You fascinate me, Charlotte, do you know that? I left behind a young, headstrong tomboy of a girl. I now find a cold, reserved woman. So——' he shrugged slightly '—I want to see what, or who, it is that makes the new Charlotte Mercer tick.'

'It's quite simple, Jude.' Somehow she managed to inject her voice with a cool indifference. 'You grow up over seven years. I'm much too old to be a tomboy.'

'Mmm, but maybe it's not that simple. Maybe, in your case, it was much more rapid than that. Like overnight, and one particular night at that—the night Simon died.'

She closed her eyes for a moment. 'Please, Jude, I don't want to talk about it.'

'Ah, but I do.' There was no trace of pity in his voice. 'What's it called—therapy? We've both surely thought about it enough, and as the two people most intimately involved, I'm afraid, Charlotte, that we're going to have to talk about it.'

They were on the motorway by now but, although the traffic was building up ahead, he shot her a quick glance and she edged instinctively a little further away from him. This was nothing, she thought miserably, like the brittle, successful small talk she had envisaged, when she had recovered from the shock of their first meeting.

'All right,' Jude went on, 'so there was enough evidence to satisfy the coroner that Simon had plenty of reason for getting blind drunk that night—his contract with the theatre not being renewed, no other work in sight, and me swanning off——' there was a self-flaying bitterness in his tone which struck even through her misery '—all set to scoop those wonderful glittering prizes. But we know that there was more, much more, to it than that, don't we, Charlotte?'

She was hardly aware now of the naked hostility in his tone; her mind was too busy grappling with the implications of his biting words. How much did he know? This question, which she had asked herself over and over again since that searing scene, when, past guilt, past grief, past anything, she had stood numbly in the churchyard as Jude, his face ravaged by pain, had stopped beside her merely long enough to fling at her those few bitter, cruel words, the question was once again clamouring for an answer. She had striven to keep the truth from Simon at all costs, so that he should not be hurt any more than was absolutely necessary, so how could Jude, above everyone, know or even suspect that it was her love for him which had in the end made it impossible for her to marry his brother?

'There was no need to tell anyone at the time, but Simon rang me that night.'

An involuntary gasp burst from her and she swung round, but Jude's eyes were fixed straight ahead.

'H-he rang you? But you were in Italy!'

'That's right. But he still rang me. I promised him that I would come home the next morning, but of course it was too late by then.' Beneath the seeming composure, she sensed the desolation. 'I decided not to say anything at the inquest. At least, then, I could spare Simon's memory the shame of everyone knowing the truth——'

Charlotte had stopped breathing. 'The—the truth?'

'That you'd thrown him over, after just a few weeks, for another man.'

Another man. Her hands tightened painfully on one another as the flood of tension burst, then ebbed inside her, leaving her weak with relief. The nightmare possibility which had haunted her for years and which had seemed about to become reality had not happened. So Simon had not guessed the truth, as she had been so terrified that he might have done, in the long watches of that night before setting out on his last crazy, drunken joyride.

The bitter irony of it all struck her, so that for a moment she had to bite back a wild laugh. Seven years before she had lied to Simon, telling him that there was someone else, as the kindest way to conceal from him that once again he had lost out to his twin. Now, somehow, she would have to tell that same lie all over again, to keep from Jude the knowledge which he, in his turn, would find totally unbearable, that it was for futile, hopeless love of him—and, in the end, even more than that, her abhorrence of betraying Simon to the ultimate degree. Somehow, whatever mental torments he might inflict on her, she would bear them and keep the remotest suspicion of that final truth from Jude, lest his quick brain leap from suspicion to deduction and certainty. His beloved twin's death had hurt him so deeply that she, even though her feelings for him were long dead, would not allow him to be hurt again.

'Who was he, this other man? Surely not Stuart Fletcher?'

Engrossed in her own complex web of thought, she hardly registered the question.

'Oh no.' Her reply was mechanical. 'I met Stuart when I went to London.'

She glanced round and fleetingly their eyes met, then hers fell before the blazing anger in his.

'Well,' Jude demanded, 'was it someone local? Someone I knew?'

'No! I mean, you didn't know him. Look,' she said loudly, injecting an anger which was not altogether counterfeit into her voice, 'it's nothing to do with you, so leave it, will you? It was someone I met after—after you'd left.'

'Why didn't you marry him?'

Oh God, would he ever stop this remorseless inquisition? She could feel beads of sweat breaking out on her forehead. She hesitated, then as the angry silence hung between them, said, 'It just didn't work out, that's all.' She was extemporising wildly. 'I thought I loved him, but I realised very soon that I was wrong and so I——'

Too late, she realised the trap she had set and sprung on herself. Jude gave a savage exclamation, braked hard and swung the car out of the stream of traffic on to the hard shoulder. She felt him move in his seat, but kept her head turned from him, watching as the driving rain formed abstract patterns like tears on the glass, until he put his hand under her chin, forcing her face towards him.

'Is that true?' he demanded. 'You aren't lying to me, are you?'

His eyes were almost black, cold and hard as obsidian, and she flinched from the expression in them. But she forced herself to meet them coolly.

'Of course I'm not. Why should I?'

Jude shook his head disbelievingly. 'My God, you threw Simon over for a passing fancy! You killed him— yes, killed him,' he said savagely, as she uttered a whimper of protest, 'and for a mere infatuation, a——' He broke off abruptly, then went on, his voice unsteady. 'I thought I knew you, Charlotte. All those years, I thought you cared about us all.'

The pain in his voice was lacerating her. Somehow, she had to stop him punishing them both. She managed a light half-shrug. 'Well, you obviously didn't know me well enough, did you?'

He stared at her for a long, endless moment, then said, his voice cold with contempt, 'No, I didn't. The Charlotte I thought I knew could never have been so casual, so uncaring—so cruel.'

He released his grip on her, started up the engine and, without another word, eased the car out into the flow of traffic. She stared straight ahead of her, past the flashing windscreen blades, the defensive retort which had sprung to her lips still trembling unsaid. It was far better this way, better for both their sakes that, however unfair, unjust it might be, he should think this of her, that he should never even for an instant suspect the truth. And yet—surreptitiously, she flicked away one tear that, sneaking past her guard, had oozed out and was trickling slowly down her cheek.

CHAPTER FOUR

'RIGHT. Out you get.'

The silence had hung heavy between them for so long that Charlotte started at the sound of Jude's voice. Slumped dejectedly, her thoughts increasingly dark and disturbing, she had hardly been aware of the London suburbs, the frenetic traffic, but now she registered that he had pulled up in a quiet, sunlit square, outside one of a row of tall Georgian town houses.

He got out and went round to the boot, then appeared on the pavement, carrying a case and with a huge cream suede, fur-lined jacket slung carelessly from his shoulders. He opened her door and repeated peremptorily, 'Out.'

Should she sit tight, mule-like, refusing point-blank to budge? Charlotte caught his eye and scrambled out hastily. She leaned against the side of the car with an assumed nonchalance which she was very far from feeling and, as he locked the door, tried without success to be unaware of the covertly amused glances her outfit was attracting from a group of smartly dressed young women. She shot Jude a baleful look, which he totally ignored, then limped after him up an imposing flight of steps and through the front door.

'Afternoon, Mr Renton, sir.'

A uniformed porter emerged from his cubbyhole, buttoning up his jacket. His eyes, straying to the dazzling yellow apparition beside Jude, widened momentarily, then he added politely, 'Good afternoon, miss.

Couple of letters upstairs for you, sir—and the wife's got some food in. Just the one night, isn't it?'

'Thanks, Cowley. Yes, one night—oh, and I'm going out again soon, so don't put the Jag away.'

Charlotte, all ears, listened to this exchange, her heart sinking lower at every word. Going out? Don't put the Jag away? Earlier, she had consoled herself with the small, comforting thought that, with a performance tonight, their visit was to be a very fleeting one, but as she squeaked disconsolately after Jude to the lift, across the miles of shiny parquet, unpleasant prickles of suspicion were niggling at her mind.

The lift was extremely small, and when Jude had dumped the case, she was forced to stand facing him so near that the soft sleeves of his coat brushed delicately against her hand, and when he turned his head slightly, she could feel his breath against her ear. She fixed her eyes firmly on the lowest button of three on his black cashmere shirt sweater, then, as she became aware of the gentle rise and fall of his chest, her glance slid hastily away to the control panel of the lift.

'Look,' she began huskily, though still without meeting his eyes, 'what's going on? Aren't you going back to Stratford tonight, and if not——' there was an increasing tremor of uncertainty in her voice, which she struggled unsuccessfully to quell '—w-what do you intend to do about me? I—I insist that you tell me!'

He raised one eyebrow mockingly. 'Insist? I don't somehow think you're in any position to insist on anything, Charlotte.'

His coolly self-possessed tone set her very teeth on edge with suppressed anger—and fear.

The lift slowed, then halted. The door, though, remained tightly closed and, for an agonising few seconds, she thought wildly that it must have jammed. Hours, perhaps a whole night, trapped in a metal box with Jude...

The door slid smoothly back and she stepped out quickly. Above them was a large skylight; they must be on the top floor. She noticed also that there was only one door leading from the deeply carpeted lobby, and he unlocked it, gesturing her past him.

'Don't entertain any ideas of slipping out tonight when I've gone.' He set down his case on the pale green, soft-piled carpet. 'There's a security device on the door and you won't get back in—at least, not without a great deal of bother for everyone.'

Charlotte, her fists clenched at her side, stared at him, then backed up against the wall, folded her arms, and said very clearly, 'For the last time, Jude Renton, tell me what's going on, or—or I'll physically attack you, I swear I will!'

He shot her a glance of coldly quizzical amusement. 'That's more like the old Charlotte! But can I remind you—as far as I can remember, that is—that you never won any of our previous fights, and I assure you I have absolutely no intention of letting you begin now.'

He walked past her and, still simmering inwardly, she followed him into a spacious kitchen, lined with luxurious pale ash units as well as a bank of such fittings as a microwave, dishwasher, large fridge-freezer, which just for a moment made her think wryly of her own small, rather dingy kitchenette, cramped and basic in the extreme.

The room was airless, and Jude unlocked a pair of double doors which led out to a small, decorative wrought-iron balcony, dotted with tubs of polyanthus. Charlotte leaned up against the sink unit, staring out at the mirror-image Georgian house on the opposite side of the square.

'Correct me if I'm wrong, but I gather you're not going back to Stratford this evening.' She could have been making polite conversation on the weather.

'That's right.' Jude spoke behind her. 'It's *Romeo* tonight, which, thank God, I'm not in. I'm booked to appear in that new late-night TV chat show——' she could hear the grimace in his voice '—my agent's idea, to publicise my latest film, which is due to hit Europe right between the eyes next week.'

'And what about me, then?' Charlotte swung round to him, her hands bunching and unbunching in the deep pockets of her cagoule. 'You had absolutely no right to forcibly bring me here!'

Jude shrugged offhandedly. 'As to that, it was merely an impulse. But, if it's any consolation, as you sulked all the way here——' he ignored her gasp of indignation '—I'm beginning to wish I'd abandoned you by the roadside.'

'It's a pity you didn't,' she snapped, 'but I'm here, aren't I, so I repeat, what are you going to do about me?'

'Well, you can come with me this evening if you want to.'

'Oh, for heaven's sake!' she burst out, then stopped just as precipitately. She would not, must not lose her temper now, or all sorts of appalling things might come hurtling out. Over the years she had learned painfully to control that temper of hers, and Jude simply must not be allowed to make her lose it now. She took a deep breath. 'How can I possibly come with you, dressed like this?'

'Well, it's hardly my fault if you choose to go about in public resembling a Daffy Duck lookalike, is it?' he said in a sweetly reasonable voice. 'But if that's all that's bothering you, I'll get some clothes sent in, and you can choose an outfit.'

Charlotte shook her head decidedly. 'No, thank you.' At least, not to go anywhere with you, she added silently. However galling it was, though, it would not pay her to alienate him totally, so she added in a slightly more conciliatory tone, 'But, on second thoughts, perhaps if you could send for an outfit for me—which of course I shall pay for—I can wear it to go to a hotel for the night, and you can pick me up in the——'

'Certainly not!' Jude's eyes narrowed. 'I haven't time to dance attendance on you. And anyway, I'm not having you wandering round London on your own. You're staying right here.'

The same irrational panic which she had experienced in the car was rising inside her again. She glanced past him towards the hall, but he intercepted her look.

'And with the security lock on, you can forget all about doing a quick exit. So just take off that—monstrosity, and I'll make some coffee.'

By way of answer, she thrust her hands even deeper into her cagoule pockets and said coldly, "I'd rather have tea—that's if it's not too much trouble.'

It seemed very warm in the kitchen, and she had to have some air, so she went over to the glass doors and pushed them further open. Behind her, she heard Jude say urgently, 'No, don't go out there, Charlotte', but very deliberately she took two or three paces across the balcony. Above her were the clouds, opposite was the row of buildings she had glimpsed earlier, while below— she glanced down, and saw beneath her very feet, through the lines of the wrought iron, tiny ant-like figures swarming on the pavements. But the pattern in the ironwork was curling itself round and round in front of her and she was going to fall towards it, through it——

She closed her eyes, just as Jude caught her, his arm sweeping around her waist, and half lifted, half dragged her back on to the *terra firma* of ceramic tiles.

'You little fool—I told you not to go out there!' He shook her angrily. 'You know you can't stand heights.' He grimaced. 'I haven't forgotten—even if you have— that time at Stratford Fair, when the Big Wheel broke down with us at the top. You screeching like a stuck pig, half throttling me—you nearly had us both out!'

Charlotte looked at him, her eyes wide. So Jude remembered. After all these years—for what had she been?—nine, certainly no more than ten—he had remembered that silly, trivial incident which she, thoroughly embarrassed by her panic-stricken be- haviour, had put from her mind with all possible speed.

'Anyway, are you OK?'

The terrible feeling of vertigo was receding and she nodded dumbly, then managed to whisper, 'Y-yes, thank you.'

Jude was holding her by both wrists, and at the touch of his warm hands on her skin she felt the colour, which had drained from her face, flooding back. They stared at each other for a time-clutching moment, then he abruptly spread his hands in a gesture of release and turned away, opening a wall cupboard to get out a teapot, cup and saucer.

'You'd better ring the police about your car,' he said over his shoulder.

'Oh, yes, thanks.' She hesitated, then said, 'I'll—I'll make another call first, if I may.'

'Feel free.' His voice was faintly ironic. 'The phone's in the sitting room through there. Help yourself.'

Like the kitchen and hall, the enormous L-shaped sitting room was beautifully furnished, and yet there was an impersonal, even anonymous air to the tasteful elegance. Jude was obviously a bird of passage here, and this apartment had nothing of him apparent in it—at least, apart from a large abstract black and white painting of a head on the far wall, its intricate, coolly distant structure perfectly matching the complex personality that lurked behind the strong, handsome face of the man in the other room.

Charlotte perched on the soft arm of a moss-green velvet upholstered easy chair and dialled the number, her eyes still fixed idly on the picture as she heard the phone ringing. Yes, that was Jude's own choice; an interior designer would have chosen something more discreet, less subtly disturbing...

'Charlotte—is that you?' Stuart's voice broke into her thoughts abruptly. 'Where the devil are you?'

He sounded extremely put out and she realised, too late, that she should have prepared for this conversation with more care. She couldn't possibly tell him all that had happened—at least, not until she was safely back in Stratford—but how could she avoid it? Prevarication, that was it.

'Well, actually, Stu, it's a long——'

'I've had the police round here! Your car's been found this afternoon, in Chipping Norton.'

'Is it all right?' she asked eagerly.

'Why shouldn't it be? But the doors were wide open and as there was a pile of our brochures in the glove compartment they got in touch with me.'

'Oh, thank goodness! I thought they might have——'

'*They?* Who are *they*? What the hell's been going on? And why did you leave the car? Look, I'm coming straight round.'

'Oh, no—no, please don't bother, Stu. Everything's fine—really. There was just a bit of a—mix-up, but there's no need for you——'

'OK. I've got one or two things to tie up here,' he agreed reluctantly, and then, just as she relaxed a fraction, 'so I'll pick you up at eight, as we'd arranged.'

Her dinner date! Oh, good grief, she'd completely forgotten that!

'No, Stu,' she put in urgently, 'I—I can't make to-night, I'm afraid. Tomorrow evening—yes, tomorrow will be fine.'

She was almost babbling in her anxiety to keep the truth from him, the fingers of her free hand beating an urgent tattoo on the low table beside her, when she heard a faint sound which just might have been a muffled snort of derision. Turning, she saw Jude, propped up in the doorway, his arms folded. She shot him a savage look, which should have felled him at ten yards, then turned back to the phone to hear Stuart saying obstinately, 'Tomorrow will not be fine. I'm coming round at eight.'

'No! No, don't—you can't——'

She broke off helplessly, then gave a gasp of outrage as Jude removed the receiver from her shaking hand and said into it, 'Fletcher? This is Jude Renton. Charlotte is with me at my flat in London. I shall be bringing her back to Stratford tomorrow, so she'll be able to put you in the picture then. Goodbye.'

There was a decisive click as he replaced the receiver, cutting out the disembodied voice at the other end. She regarded him, stormy-eyed. He had, of course, done it

quite deliberately—had cynically chosen his words for
the maximum effect on Stuart, leaving him with the
clearest possible idea of what was, in truth, the opposite
of the real situation, and leaving her to extricate herself
from it as best she could.

'How dare you! That was supposed to be a private
call!'

'Oh, sorry.' He gave her a totally unrepentant smile.
'I just came in to tell you that your tea was ready, and
as you seemed to be having a slight—er—problem, I
thought I'd help you out. I gather your car's turned up.'

'Yes, at——' Charlotte stopped dead, her jaw
dropping with astonished anger. On the phone, the
tension of coping with Stuart's belligerence had meant
that the full import of his words had not immediately
registered, but now her lips tightened.

She threw him a smouldering look. 'Well? Don't you
want to know where it was found?'

'If it's not a state secret.'

His tone of total uninterest inflamed her further. 'It
was at Chipping Norton. It's quite amusing really, isn't
it,' she went on bitterly, thinking aloud. 'It was no doubt
already there, when you drove past like a bat out of hell.
Just a few minutes' delay, that's all I asked. I could have
picked it up, driven back to Stratford, and Stu—no one
would have been any the wiser. But no——' her sense
of acute grievance notched her voice up half an octave
'—you had to—to kidnap me, drag me down here like
some—some tinpot mobster——'

Too late, she saw him frown, saw his mouth tighten,
and she stopped dead. She took a step back from him,
but he caught her by the arms and shook her, his fingers
digging in, even through the PVC, before releasing his
hold and pushing her roughly away from him.

'I'm warning you—stop acting like a fishwife!' His voice was level enough, but he was obviously controlling his temper with difficulty. 'And as for kidnapping you, don't be so childish. If—when I do kidnap you, Charlotte——' was there, just for a moment, a glint of very private amusement in those unrevealing blue eyes? '—it will be a professional job, I promise you.'

As she stared mutinously up at him, he went on, 'And now, take that ridiculous outfit off, while I fetch in your tea.'

When he had gone, Charlotte sat down on the sofa and very gingerly eased off one wellington, wincing as it caught on the blister, dragging the skin away to expose a raw, inflamed area that throbbed violently as she gently probed the flesh around it. She pulled the other boot off, then, with a groan of relief, stood up, her feet sinking gratefully into the dense carpet, and began tugging off her cagoule. But in her haste to be free of it before Jude returned, she wrenched impatiently at the zip, jamming it less than half open.

She was still wrestling in an ineffectual frenzy with it, her head completely trapped, when she heard Jude's voice say impatiently, 'Oh, for heaven's sake! Keep still,' and his hands were deftly easing the narrow opening past her ears. A moment later she felt herself free, but then, as she straightened up with an involuntary sigh of relief, brushing her dishevelled hair from her face, she glanced down and gasped with horrified embarrassment. That last, long tug had certainly removed her cagoule—but it had also peeled her out of her pink T-shirt as neatly as a banana skin, leaving the curve of her delicately rounded breasts now all too apparent in the low-cut lace bra.

For a moment, slowly, almost reluctantly, Jude's gaze roved over her creamy white skin, and she stood motionless, her head bent and one hand clutched across her in an instinctive gesture as she felt her skin treacherously take fire under the touch of his eyes. Then, with a quick movement, he disentangled her T-shirt and thrust it at her.

'Put it on.'

His voice was harsh, and when she dared to shoot him a covert glance, she saw his mouth was set in a grim line. She mumbled her thanks, then, turning her back, wriggled into the shirt, not tucking it in, but leaving it loose, so that it masked rather than accentuated the lines of her slender figure.

Over her shoulder, to hide her confusion, she said, as casually as her still-erratic heart beat would allow, 'I— I gather this is your flat?'

'Yes—although I'm rarely here. My parents get more use out of it than I do, but I need a London base for when I'm over from the States, and I don't much care for hotels. It's as simple as that.'

'I see.' She desperately wanted to ask how his parents— Mrs Renton, in particular—were, but the question would not come. Their well-being was a part of the whole monstrous taboo area that lay between them.

Jude had set the tea tray on a side table and she saw now that it held only one cup and saucer.

'I'll leave you to it, while I get ready. I'm due at the studio in an hour or so.' Jude's voice still held a disturbing harshness, and without waiting for her reply, he turned on his heel and walked out.

Charlotte poured herself a cup of tea, took a couple of her favourite chocolate wholemeal biscuits and leaned morosely against the back of the plush sofa. She drained the cup, set it down with hands which were still inclined to be unsteady, then knelt, her chin on her arms, idly watching the rush-hour traffic in the square below. She should be at home now, getting ready for her date with Stuart, whereas, thanks to Jude's bloody-mindedness, and the fates which had impelled her to leave her car unlocked and then reach the main road at the precise moment that—— She gave a faint, rueful smile. Perhaps, after all, it had been the Whispering Knights—or the Witch of Rollright herself—that she had heard, plotting her imminent destruction . . .

> Rise up, stick, and stand still, stone,
> For King of England thou shalt be none;
> Thou and thy men hoarstones shall be
> And I myself an eldern tree.

. . . The words of the ancient spell echoed disturbingly in her mind, but she was almost grateful for it, drowning out as it did alarming thoughts which would keep edging into her consciousness, thoughts which centred on Jude—and on her reaction to that casual touch of his hand on her flesh, that look in his eyes, unwilling, angry even, as she stood before him. In spite of the warm sunshine streaming into the room, she shivered. Just what might some malevolent fate be holding in store for her, now that once again she and Jude had been brought together? And would this seemingly accidental encounter, appalling as it was, merely be a passing, ephemeral phase in her life, or would it prove to be the opening act of a drama as potent as any tragedy that he would ever perform in?

She did not hear the door open, but from behind her, she realised, with a swift tensing of her stomach muscles, Jude was reflected in the window pane, and she turned very slowly, unwilling to meet his eye. He had shaved, and his hair was still slightly damp from his shower. He had also replaced the casual black cords and sweater with a pale grey suit in some beautiful lightweight fabric, a white shirt and silvery grey tie. He looked quite devastatingly handsome, and as her eyes took in first his body, then his face, a heavy band seemed to settle painfully down across her ribs, so that she could scarcely breathe, the heaviness composed of sadness, anger, desolation, and another, even more basic feeling to which she dared not put a name.

Thrown completely off balance, she took refuge in attack. Raising her brows, she said, with an unmistakable waspishness in her voice, 'Oh, very fetching. Your admirers will be knocked all of a heap!'

'What would you have preferred me to wear?' Jude's tone was cold. 'Yellow oilskins?'

Charlotte opened her mouth, but then closed it on the quick retort which had sprung to her lips. Petty sniping at a man like Jude was altogether too dangerous. She must be careful—they were both obviously on a short fuse, she because she had been swept totally out of her depth, and Jude—well, she could not begin to guess what thoughts were circulating through his devious mind.

'Anyway,' he went on, 'I'm not some teenage rock star—my fans expect me to be well dressed, so——' he shrugged '—being a very sensible man, I oblige them.' He glanced at his watch. 'I must go. Make yourself at home—the bathroom's through there. There's plenty of food, so get yourself a meal. Or if you'd prefer, I'll get Cowley to fetch you in a Chinese takeaway—there's a good one round the corner.'

'Oh no, thank you.' She uncurled herself from the sofa and stood up, uncertainly fingering the clasp on her jeans. That dull ache was spreading all through her body now, and she just wanted him to go, so that finally she could be alone. 'Well, good luck. I must say,' she managed a faint smile, 'you're very cool for someone who's about to be mauled on a live chat show in front of millions!'

Jude began to say something, but stopped abruptly and said instead, 'Oh, I dare say. I might even enjoy this particular mauling, and anyway, my agent's told me I've got to be on my best behaviour.'

He paused in the doorway. 'And remember, don't attempt to leave the flat.' The warning in his tone was perfectly clear.

CHAPTER FIVE

CHARLOTTE leaned against the window, watching until Jude had got into the car and driven off. Now that he actually had gone, the flat felt very empty, even alien, as though she were an unwelcome intruder. She scolded herself angrily. After all, it was Jude's fault, not hers, if she had been foisted on to his territory. What she needed was food. Well, he was right in that respect—there was plenty of food, she realised, as she opened the freezer and surveyed the steak, chops, and individual portions of duck à l'orange.

In the end, though, feeling lazy, she settled for a ploughman's—though a ploughman with a difference, she thought, as she examined the contents of the cheese compartment: Stilton, Brie, Roquefort and a carton of delicious-looking soft, herb-speckled cheese. She took some of each, cut a large hunk of granary bread—like the cheeses, from a Top People's food hall—and filled up the plate with some ready-prepared salad. She ate at the kitchen table, then made a cup of coffee and carried it into the sitting-room.

She wandered across to the window. In the luminous air of a fine spring evening, the tiny figures below her seemed to move with a jaunty step, while only she was trapped up here, isolated, forced to wait until Jude chose to return... She drank her coffee, flicking through the couple of evening papers which had appeared silently on the hall rug. Some glossy magazines lay on the coffee table, and she thumbed through them desultorily until she came face to face with yet another article on Jude Renton, then tossed them aside hastily and began to pace the room. She glanced at the digital clock on the low mantelpiece. Seven o'clock. The chat show did not even begin for another four hours—an endless evening stretched before her.

Gripped by nervous uncertainty, and quite unable to sit still, she continued her restless padding about the room. Up, down, across... Fifty times, until she stumbled into the coffee table, banging her sore heel. When she examined the blister, she saw that some grains of dirt had lodged in it. Perhaps a bath would help—at any rate, that would pass away a couple of boring hours, and it might even do something for her rapidly fraying nerve ends—although she rather doubted it. Those nerve ends were unravelling solely in tense expectation of Jude's return, and she could do nothing about that.

In the beautiful champagne-tiled bathroom, she discovered a whirlpool bath—she'd always wanted to try one. She set the water running, then, as she straightened up, realised that before he'd left, Jude had not shown her his spare bedroom. The first door she tried obviously led into his room, his case open on the large double bed, a hint of his expensive after-shave hanging in the air.

She hastily closed the door again, a faint frown of puzzlement on her face. The front door...the kitchen...bathroom...the two doors into the sitting-room...behind her, Jude's bedroom. There was no other door. There was no spare room. It was a one-bedroomed apartment. In that case... Charlotte swallowed as the nervous intensity she had been feeling all evening tightened into a spasm of dread. In that case, just where did he intend her to——

The sound of water roused her and she flew back to
the bathroom, just in time. There was a bottle of oil
beside the bath and she poured in a generous portion,
then, still abstractedly, shed her clothes, climbed in and
lay back in the rippling water. It was a marvellously sen-
suous feeling, as though she were being stroked gently
all over by soothing, cosseting hands, and when, after
far too long, she finally sat up, her entire body was so
deeply relaxed that she could scarcely heave herself out.

It was far too much bother to dress again, and Jude
would still not be back for hours, so she wrapped herself
in the black towelling robe that was hanging on the back
of the door, then tottered back to the sitting-room. She
piled every cushion on to the sofa, then, for good
measure, fetched the four pillows from Jude's bed—she
must just ensure that they were returned to base before
he arrived—switched on the television and collapsed as
though into a downy nest, one slim, throbbing foot suspended over the edge...

The door opened and, before she could quite jump
out of her skin in terror, the wall light snapped on and
Jude was standing in the doorway, his jacket draped
casually over one arm. She lay blinking up at him for
one dazed instant, then, as she saw his eyes darken, her
own dropped in confusion and she realised that, sprawled
as she was among the cushions, the robe was revealing
considerably more of her pale, creamy skin than it was
hiding.

She clutched it to her as he went across and switched
off the television, then tossed his jacket down on a chair,
unhooking his tie with one finger. He came over to the
sofa and stood, regarding her, while she lay very still,
all too conscious that it would be a grave error to attempt to struggle even into a sitting position. Beyond

him, she was aware of the papers and magazines strewn across the floor, her dirty coffee cup still over by the window where she had abandoned it, and one of his pillows, which had fallen to the floor. She flushed with mortification.

'I'm sorry—about the mess, I mean,' she began, but Jude silenced her with a wave of the hand. He picked up the pillow and threw it down beside her.

'Don't give it a thought. After all,' his voice was dry, 'I did tell you to make yourself thoroughly at home. It's just that I'd forgotten what an untidy little slob you always were.'

Her lips tightened, not so much at the insult, which was surely deserved, but at the careless way he had tossed it at her.

'I'm very sorry,' she said, with an attempt at haughtiness. 'I meant to clear up before you came back, but I must have gone off to sleep. I've missed your programme.'

Jude was gathering up newspapers and magazines. 'Oh, didn't I tell you? Sorry.' She caught the glint of a smile in his eyes. 'It was pre-recorded—it isn't on for another hour. But I wouldn't bother. Not one of my award-winning performances.' He grimaced. 'I rather lost my cool, I'm afraid.'

'You lost your cool!' She stared at him in genuine amazement. 'How on earth did you do that?'

'Oh—you know,' he shrugged impatiently. 'That bloody presenter—he started asking questions deliberately meant to be provocative. So he got what he was after—I was provoked.'

'Your agent won't be pleased, not after you'd promised to behave yourself.'

'Oh, I don't know.' His tone was grim. 'I'll no doubt make the front pages of the tabloids tomorrow, so that'll keep him happy.'

'But what did he say?' Charlotte persisted, curiosity driving her further, beyond the caution which common sense told her would be preferable, given the simmering fury still all too evident within Jude.

'It doesn't matter. Just leave it, will you?'

He spoke through tight lips, then turned away as though to end the exchange. She risked another furtive look at him, seeing his face dark with brooding anger, an anger which she knew for once was not directed against her. Someone had foolishly—or, she thought, much more likely, *deliberately*—set out to push Jude just a little too far.

As if making a conscious effort to shake himself free of his black mood, he asked abruptly, 'How's your blister, by the way?'

'Oh, it's fine,' she said hastily.

But he came across and squatted down on his haunches beside the sofa. She went to move the foot out of his reach but, ignoring her protestations, he caught hold of it and his long, sensitive fingers probed around with a gentle touch which she scarcely felt. She leaned back, studying surreptitiously the strong lines of his half-averted face as he bent over her foot. He was frowning in concentration, and she saw the faint, bruised shadows brushed under his eyes, which gave him, for a few moments at any rate, a transient vulnerability. Of course, she knew that it was purely a deceptive vulnerability—at least—her throat constricted painfully—deceptive as far as she was concerned. And yet, in spite of herself, somewhere in the pit of her stomach a quite dreadful, desolate ache of longing stirred like some insidious serpent, a longing to lean forward...touch him... A fine tremor ran through her whole body, and Jude's fingers stilled.

'Am I hurting you?'

'N-no.'

He must have caught something of her inner turmoil in the huskily uttered word, for he glanced up swiftly. Their eyes caught and locked in an endless moment of time, and dimly Charlotte was aware of his fingers tightening their grip on her, then brusquely he released her foot so that it fell back on the cushion, and straightened up.

'I'm afraid you've still got quite a bit of dirt in it. It must be got out or you'll end up with an infection.' His voice was devoid of expression, and he turned away abruptly.

She still had not recovered her poise when he returned with a bowl of warm water and some cotton wool, and as he knelt in front of her again she kept her head lowered, her fingers nervously twining among the tasselled cord of the robe.

'Does it hurt?'

She knew his eyes were on her face, but she could not steel herself to meet that intent, sapphire gaze.

'No,' she murmured. In fact, the pain was raw, quite out of proportion to one stupid blister, but though she felt beads of sweat breaking out on her upper lip, somehow she fiercely willed herself to bear the discomfort without flinching, as though, by so doing, she would punish her body for its earlier weakness.

When he had finished, Jude patted her foot dry, then smeared on antiseptic cream and finally slipped on a large grey sock.

'One of mine, but don't alarm yourself,' he remarked conversationally. 'I haven't got foot-and-mouth disease or anything.'

Momentarily, their eyes met again and, with a sudden leap of recognition, Charlotte saw in his that same almost imperceptible yet unmistakable wariness that, she was sure, was in her own. Quite unable to respond to his almost bantering tone, she muttered her thanks, then turned away.

'Yes, there's no need for you to worry. I'll return you, all in one piece, to Stuart's loving arms—although,' his tone switched without warning to an undisguised sneer, 'from the look of him, I'd say all he can offer is a pretty cold embrace.'

Taken completely unawares, she swung round to face him, shocked out of her flimsy hold on composure.

'Well, I'm right, aren't I?'

His cold voice mocked her and she could not reply. Deliberately, he put out a hand, and she jerked back away from him, but then, agonisingly conscious that the robe was slipping revealingly from her shoulders, she forced herself to lie passive, allowing him to tilt her face to meet his implacable gaze. He stared at her unsmiling as the colour ebbed, then flooded into her cheeks, until, with a dismissive gesture, he released her.

'There's no need to answer—I can see the truth in your face. My God, Charlotte, how could you get mixed up with a cold fish like that?'

Because he was the exact opposite of you, every fibre in her wanted to scream out. But instead, clenching her hands until the knuckles whitened, she willed herself to return his contemptuous look with frozen hauteur.

'You don't know Stuart, so don't presume to judge him.'

'Well, if you're so fond of Stuart,' he mimicked her voice savagely, 'why aren't you married to him? You're not living with him, I know, so——'

She stared at him blankly. 'How on earth do you know that?'

He shrugged. 'Oh, you know Stratford. It's a small place. Nobody has any secrets there for long.'

But Charlotte wasn't fooled. 'You've been prying into my life,' she said slowly. 'How—how dare you!'

She struggled desperately for self-control, but the anger which she had held rigorously on a choke chain ever since her enforced journey to London kindled and exploded into blazing life.

'You—you——' She raised her clenched fist to strike him, but Jude caught her roughly by the wrist, wrenching her arm down again, and as she swore at him he put his other hand across her mouth to silence her.

'Well, well! I was beginning to wonder what had happened to that celebrated temper of yours. So it's not dead, after all, but sleeping, as they say. I wonder what else,' he went on musingly, 'of the old Charlotte is still there for the finding, beneath that cold crust—if you dig deep enough.'

All at once, whether he realised it or not, they were on a frighteningly treacherous ground once more, and if she did not control her tongue they could both be sucked into the shadowy quicksands of their past. Cursing herself for her self-indulgent folly in allowing Jude, still smarting from his television encounter, to provoke her in his turn to reckless fury, Charlotte pulled herself together with a gigantic effort.

'I've told you,' she said carefully, 'my—*our* private life has nothing to do with you—nothing at all. So, please, just leave me alone.'

In spite of herself, her voice caught slightly on the final word. Somehow there was a rank treachery in even allowing Stuart's name to be mentioned by Jude, and this feeling piled itself on to the guilt she already felt over Stuart ... It was he who had wanted them to marry when they'd first arrived in Stratford; she who had inexplicably dragged her feet, suggesting first midsummer and then, as a final date, the end of their first tourist season...and it was she who had refused to move in with him, she who always ...

She dragged herself out of this depressing and unprofitable train of thought and, in an effort to break the tension that was threatening to enmesh them both, she glanced at the clock and said coldly, 'It's nearly time for your programme. I presume you don't want to miss it.'

As he made no response, she went to get up, but before she could move he stretched out one arm across her stomach, pinning her back against the sofa.

'No, you're not watching it, I'm afraid, Charlotte.'

She stared at him in astonishment. 'But I want to! I——'

Jude shook his head with a finality that infuriated her. 'Sorry, but what you want doesn't come into it, on this occasion.'

Or on any other occasion, she thought bitterly. A flicker of amusement momentarily lightened the steel in his eyes and she realised, with a spurt of self-irritated chagrin, that he was fully aware of that last private thought.

'Don't tell me,' she injected her voice with heavy sarcasm, 'that the great Jude Renton's ashamed of his unedifying performance!' And heedless of the warning tightening of his lips into a thin line, of the way his outflung hand curled into itself, as though barely subduing the urge to seize and shake her she rushed on, repeating stubbornly, 'Anyway, I want to see it, even if you don't. I want to see just what it took to make you lose that beautifully controlled temper of yours.'

'Don't push me, Charlotte. For the last time, you are *not* watching that programme. So you either accept that, or——'

The undisguised menace in his voice silenced her, and she had just enough self-control to draw back. It was clear that Jude, for whatever reason, was determined that she would not get her way, and therefore, however galling it might be for her, it was pointless to prolong this unequal confrontation.

'Very well, then,' she said, 'it's been a very tiring day. I'll go to bed.'

Jude's arm relaxed its hold and he stood up. 'Very sensible. After all, we'll be making an early start in the morning.'

Charlotte had half risen from the sofa when she stopped.

'Now what's the matter? Oh, of course, the bedroom— it's through there.' He gestured casually towards the door.

'Y-yes, I know,' she stammered, furiously aware of the colour rising in her cheeks. 'But—but that's yours— and there isn't another bedroom, so——'

'So you've already checked on that.' His eyes glittered in open amusement. 'But that's no problem—be my guest.'

She got up, adjusting the belt of the robe with shaking hands. 'As you haven't a spare room to accommodate unexpected—guests——' 'prisoners' had almost slipped out, but she bit it back and went on, with all of the little dignity she could summon '—perhaps you'd be good enough to ring your obliging Mr Cowley. In a large place like this, there's sure to be an empty flat I can use overnight.'

'Sorry.' Jude shook his head firmly. 'I've already told you, I'm not letting you out of this place. True, there is an empty flat on the floor below, but you're staying right here.'

She scowled up at him, then snatched up an armful of cushions and hurled them across the room in the general direction of their respective armchairs.

'In that case,' she said between her teeth, and grabbed another two cushions, skimming them past Jude's head as near as she dared without actually hitting him, 'perhaps you'll find me a couple of blankets—that's if it isn't too much bother for you.'

She carefully arranged two of the pillows from Jude's bed at one end of the sofa. It would not be too bad a night—the sofa was wide and beautifully soft and, besides, the constant sparring with Jude and the build-up of nervous tension it had generated in her had left her all at once drained and utterly exhausted so that she felt she could have slept dreamlessly on a clothesline.

'Certainly not. I won't hear of you dossing down out here, while I'm reclining at my ease in a luxurious double bed.'

Charlotte stared at him. He was playing with her, she was almost sure of that. But why was he still prolonging this game of cat and mouse, which was so hateful to her and must surely be distasteful to him? He hated her, he'd made that perfectly clear, and yet...there had never been anything petty or mean-minded about Jude, and surely he was too big a man now, in every sense of the word, merely to be getting some cheap amusement out of her discomfiture.

She shook her head slightly in puzzlement. He and
Simon had so often indulged themselves in teasing her—
Jude much less often than Simon, but even so, when he
had had a certain mood of devilment on him... But
now, years on, the harmless childhood baiting had assumed an added, dangerous dimension, and Jude's
sniping seemed to be taking a scarcely veiled sexual turn.
But surely he, even feeling for her the way he did, could
not be that cruel? The memory of their secret, shared
afternoon in that sweetly scented conservatory—always
with her but never more potent than now, in this enforced intimacy with him—he could not possibly have
put it from him completely, however much he might have
striven to do so.

As she looked at him, she saw that he was watching
her and, for a moment, the grim lines around his mouth
softened slightly into the faintest of smiles.

'OK, Charlotte, you can relax. The bed's all yours.
You've appropriated my bathrobe, without so much as
a by your leave—though I must admit,' his dark eyes
skimmed her from head to toe, 'it's never looked quite
as fetching on me——' colour flared into her cheeks and
she looked away, at least as ill at ease at the hardly per-
ceptible undercurrent in his voice, as during their recent
skirmishing '—so you may as well appropriate the bed
as well.'

He put a hand on her arm and steered her, feet
dragging unwillingly across the carpet, to his room. She
wanted to tell him that she couldn't possibly sleep in his
bed, that wild horses wouldn't drag her into it, alive or
dead, but somehow she was standing there meekly in the
middle of the cream Chinese embossed rug as Jude
hunted through the chest of drawers. He took out a pair
of navy pyjamas and tossed them at her.

'You can have these.' He hesitated, then lifted out another pair. 'I usually sleep in the raw, but out of deference to your sensibilities, I'll wear these tonight, even if I am safely in the other room.'

When Charlotte came back from the bathroom, he was reaching down a quilt from the fitted wardrobe. 'The sofa folds down into a bed, so you needn't lie awake worrying—I'll be quite comfortable,' he remarked. 'Well, get into bed, then.'

When she continued to stand, her fingers plucking at the bathrobe, which she had put on again, enveloping herself tightly in it as though in some kind of defensive skin, he gave an irritable exclamation, then, with one quick, decisive gesture, untied the robe and pulled it from her.

For a moment, he looked down at her, taking in the over-long sleeves, the rolled-up legs, then turned away to pick up the quilt.

'For heaven's sake, get into bed, will you?'

He sounded angry again about something and Charlotte, quite unable to face any more scenes—whether of her own or his making—hastened to obey. She lay quietly in bed, like a well-behaved child, as Jude pulled the covers up around her, and when he said a perfunctory 'goodnight' she could only mumble, ''Night.'

When he had switched off the light and closed the door, though, she lay rigid, listening to the sounds as he moved about in the adjoining room, until the faint light shining under the door went out abruptly. She should feel angry, she knew—angry that Jude had so ruthlessly taken her over, completely disregarding her protests and wishes—and yet, creeping over her stealthily in the darkness like a warm tide, came an utterly ridiculous feeling of total happiness. She was lying in Jude's bed, and he—he was nearby if she needed him, wanted him—— Oh, God! She stretched out her arm and fumbled for the bedside light, then lay staring up at the ceiling, as the happiness was blotted out by raw panic.

Instead of thinking of Stuart, as she should have been, upset, worried, not knowing what was going on, she had been—— She broke off the train of thought, biting her lip until tears started to her eyes. And it was worse, far worse than that, she thought miserably. She couldn't even see Stuart any more; he was already fading away from her like an almost forgotten dream at daybreak, paling into an insubstantial shadow which she could not seize on...

She rolled on to her side, closed her eyes tight and began desperately trying to conjure up a blueprint of the features that made up Stuart's face, but long after she had switched off the light and was finally drifting off to sleep, another face, arrogant, angry, cruel even, was still filling her whole mind, the mocking lips seeming to whisper to her, 'You see, you can't escape me, Charlotte.'

She put her hands up to her ears and said aloud into the darkness, 'Leave me alone. Oh, leave me alone! What do you want from me?'

CHAPTER SIX

CHARLOTTE roused reluctantly the next morning, but she came to with a start when she heard sounds of movement from the next room. She pushed back the bedclothes and went to peep out of the window, but then, as purposeful footsteps approached her door, she took a flying leap back into bed, curling down into it just as Jude gave a perfunctory knock and came in.

She watched him over the curve of quilt as he set down a cup of tea beside her, then turned away to draw back the heavy curtains. He was already dressed, in the same outfit as the previous afternoon, the black sweater rippling under the broad strength of his shoulders, the tight black cords revealing the graceful line of his slim hips and long legs.

Without warning, a vivid recollection came to her of a scene long buried beneath the surface of her consciousness. One broiling hot summer day, when the twins had been about seventeen, she had stumbled on them over at the old swimming pool in the Manor grounds. She had stood, half hidden by a sprawling rhododendron bush, suddenly overcome by a shyness she had been too young to understand as, stripped naked, they had tumbled in and out of the brackish water, tossing back rainbows of spray from their hair as the water glistened on their bronzed bodies. She remembered how, for an instant, and filled with new, strange and disturbing emotions, she had stared at Jude, very much as though he had been the reincarnation of some young

god, come back to earth—and then Mrs Renton had appeared and bundled her quickly away, to see if the
cherries were ripe in the orchard...

'I've got to be back in Stratford this morning,' Jude
said over his shoulder, 'so when you've had your tea,
can you get a move on? The bathroom's all yours.'

Charlotte was grateful for the brusqueness of his tone,
which clearly did not invite any response, and when he
had gone she drank down the hot tea almost without
noticing it, then got out of bed and went through the
connecting door to the bathroom. Jude was obviously
in a tearing hurry to be away—the smell of toast was
already wafting through to her. And she too was all at
once almost frantic to be away—away from a man who
was beginning to arouse ambivalent, even frightening
feelings in her, feelings that she had gratefully turned
away from for ever. In just a few hours, she told herself,
she would be safely back with the straightforward, un-
complicated Stuart.

'I love Stuart,' she said firmly to the misty reflection
in the bathroom mirror, 'and I'm going to marry him.'

She put on her jeans and T-shirt and went into the
kitchen, where Jude was sitting at the table. He poured
a glass of cold orange juice and pushed it across to her,
followed by a rack of toast.

'Coffee or tea?'

Charlotte slipped into her seat and looked across at
the black ceramic coffee pot at his elbow.

'Well, I don't mind coffee——'

'For God's sake, if you want tea, you can have tea!'

He pushed back his chair and went across to switch
on the kettle. Silence was once more clearly called for,
so she merely sipped her orange—freshly prepared, she
realised. Jude might be in a tearing hurry, she thought

a shade ironically, but he was not going to forgo the little luxuries in life.

He put down the teapot beside her. 'Sorry to get you up so early, but I really do have to get back.'

'Oh, that's all right—I was awake anyway.' The apology, grudging as it was, deserved some response. 'And there'll be plenty for me to catch up with in the office.'

'Hmm,' he eyed her thoughtfully for a moment, but then went on, 'We're having a few problems with one of the Coriolanus-Aufidius fights, so this morning I'm meeting up with Rod Farmer—he's playing Coriolanus— to try and sort them out.'

'But I thought *Coriolanus* was already in the repertoire. Shouldn't you be rehearsing for *Antony and Cleopatra* by now?'

'We are,' he said briefly, 'but this fight sequence is making a mess of the climax, so we want to get it right.'

Since her schooldays, Charlotte had always been an avid theatregoer—until this Stratford season, that was. She had stubbornly turned down all Stuart's efforts to persuade her to go to a performance, despite his argument that it was a vital part of his 'see and be seen' policy, and even when Anything Goes had received two complimentary tickets she had not changed her mind and he had taken Debbie instead. Nevertheless, in other circumstances, she would have been fascinated to ask Jude about the technicalities of the problem that had arisen and how they planned to correct it, but she was relieved when he asked abruptly,

'How's your foot, by the way?'

'Oh, it's fine. That antiseptic cream did the trick.'

Charlotte tried to smile naturally at him, but her tone was stilted. It seemed so strange, somehow, and yet so totally right to be sitting here, opposite Jude, looking at him across a jar of lime marmalade, almost as though... Her hand shook and she spilt a little of her tea as she set down the cup. What in the world was she thinking of? Mentally she should be keeping Jude at the farthest possible distance, cool, aloof, wary, not fantasising like some moony teenager.

She got up abruptly and began noisily bundling china into the sink, when Jude's impatient voice stopped her. 'Don't bother with that. Mrs Cowley will be up later, and we're leaving in precisely ten minutes.'

Once in the car, the mantle of reserve settled on him again, and when she sneaked a sideways look at his face it was set in hard, even morose lines. Conversation of any kind, even of the most superficial kind, was obviously barred, and Charlotte was highly grateful when, temporarily held up at traffic lights, he flicked through the tapes and then put one on. The haunting, wistful poignancy of Vaughan Williams' 'On Wenlock Edge' filled the car, sweet and yet with an almost unbearable sadness to it that caught her by the throat and brought burning tears to her eyes, so that she sat with head averted, watching the London streets slide past.

As the miles between her and Stratford rapidly diminished, she became increasingly preoccupied with the reception committee that was no doubt awaiting her, and was content, even grateful, for the silence to continue, both seemingly wrapped in their own very separate thoughts. Jude only transferred his intense concentration on his driving long enough to slot in one tape after another, as though pointedly to reinforce his complete disinclination for any kind of conversation with her.

When, silently ignoring her request to be dropped at the end of her street, he finally drew up outside her flat, Charlotte seized her bag and scrambled out without even the most perfunctory of goodbyes. It was, she thought, as though they were both in trembling haste to be rid of one another...

Her flat, she saw almost with astonishment, was exactly as she had left it the previous morning. Well, of course, there was no earthly reason why it should not have been. She dumped her bag and cagoule on the hall chair, picked up a circular from the doormat, and went slowly through to the kitchen. She kicked off the hated wellingtons and filled the kettle to make herself a drink before she faced Stuart and whatever else was waiting for her at Anything Goes. Then, while she waited for it to boil, she leaned against the sink, her arms folded across her chest, staring down the narrow strip of lawn.

She felt as though she had been away, not for twenty-four hours, but for months, and now she had that same slightly disorientated sensation, she thought dispassionately, which one has after returning home after a long absence, a feeling of almost frightening strangeness, before the old familiarity and security returns.

She banged her fists violently down on the sink edge, bruising her knuckles, though she hardly noticed. Damn Jude! she thought fiercely. He had done it. Only he possessed that terrible power to disturb her and set her adrift among strange emotions. A five-minute encounter at the Birthday Lunch had been enough to drive her, prowling and restless, into the Manor grounds...that split-second meeting in the ballroom had sent her fleeing, not only from Jude, but—she acknowledged this for the very first time—from herself. And now—she straightened up and switched off the kettle. She did not want a drink. She had to get out of this silent flat.

In her bedroom she tore off her jeans, dragged on the first sweater and skirt that came to hand, then snatched up her bag and almost ran out of the house.

Debbie was alone in the office, and her blue eyes lit up with vivid curiosity when she walked in. To forestall her, Charlotte said briskly, 'Hi, everything all right? Where's Stuart?'

She plumped her bag purposefully down on the desk and picked up the handful of letters lying in the in-tray, apparently finding them of engrossing interest.

'Hello, Charlotte. Stuart's got an appointment—he said tell you that your car's in the backyard. Oh, and the police want to see you.'

Her car! Temporarily, she had all but forgotten about it—the catalyst that had set in train all the previous day's traumatic events. She groaned.

'Oh, lord, I'd better go round now, I suppose, and then——'

'And Stuart said he's sure you haven't forgotten,' momentarily, there was an unconscious inflection of the same sarcasm which doubtless Stuart had used, 'but that Australian teachers' group is arriving at midday——' Charlotte hastily suppressed another groan '—and can you pick them up at the station?'

She flashed the girl a smile that brimmed with super-efficiency. 'Yes, will do, Debbie.' She looked at her watch. 'In fact, if I leave now, I can call off at the police station on my way.' She picked up her bag again. ''Bye. If I'm not back later, tell Stu I'll—well, I'll ring.'

She was already at the door when Debbie said, 'Hey, you know Jude Renton, don't you?'

Charlotte stopped in mid-flight, her hand on the door jamb. 'Well, sort of,' she admitted warily. What had Stuart been saying? she wondered, then suppressed a violent start as the girl went on, 'Did you see him on the Adrian Hadley Show last night?'

'No—no, I didn't. Er—was it good?'

Debbie rolled her eyes. 'It was great. They nearly had a punch-up!'

A punch-up! Charlotte gaped at her in horror. She'd gathered that Jude's guest appearance had not exactly been all sweetness and light, but——

'What on earth was it all about?'

'We-ell, it was funny. Nothing, really,' Debbie said reflectively. 'Hadley kept trying to find out about his love life—you know he always does—and Jude Renton was fine—"If I had a hundred pounds for all the affairs I'm supposed to have had" and so on—but then Hadley asked him, were the rumours about his relationship with Claudia Wexford true, and Jude went very uptight and said, "Oh, and what rumours did you have in mind?" in a really nasty voice. And then Hadley said, "Well, that your affair is over, and that she's been having a secret liaison with someone else for ages." Then Jude went very pale—you could see that—tore off his microphone and walked off. I don't know why he blew his top like that—even if he has split with Claudia Wexford, there'll be a queue a mile long to take her place. I certainly wouldn't——'

Charlotte looked at her watch. 'Must go now, Debbie, or I'll be late for that group. Goodbye', and she was gone.

For the next few weeks Charlotte was thankful to be extremely busy as the holiday season blossomed along with the chestnut trees in town. Although much of her time was taken up with escorting individuals and parties around the various tourist attractions, whenever possible she treated the area round the Theatre as though it were a restricted plague zone. When, unavoidably, she had to pass nearby, she walked about almost on tiptoe, camouflaged by groups of visitors or by a large, Garboish felt hat, which Stuart detested. But Jude, mercifully, remained invisible, locked no doubt into endless rehearsals for *Antony and Cleopatra*. This was to provide the vehicle for his main role for the season, and the anticipation of his performance was already capturing most of the pre-production publicity.

Her mind frequently returned to what Debbie had told her. Now that she thought back to Jude's return to his apartment following that disastrous television show, she realised what she had been half aware of at the time—that his still-smouldering anger was directed as much against himself as anyone else. And no wonder! His behaviour had hardly matched up to the carefully nurtured image of the smoothly self-confident Jude Renton of the popular papers and glossy magazines—allowing himself to be needled over the supposed end of a love affair. Perhaps the rumours were true and the affair with Claudia Wexford really was over—or perhaps, at least, she was tiring of him. But surely not—no woman would ever tire of Jude Renton.

It was Charlotte's idea that they should go to the charity event billed as 'Poetry and Music for a Summer Evening' which was to be held in the garden of a Cotswold manor house some ten miles from Stratford.

'Well, I only hope I enjoy it,' was Stuart's reaction. 'I don't usually go for poetry, and Elizabethan madrigals aren't exactly my idea of a wild night out. Besides, it'll probably rain.'

'Oh, but Stu,' Charlotte coaxed, 'a lovely setting like that, and the weather's set fair. And besides, I've already bought the tickets. But if you really don't want to go——'

'I didn't exactly say that. All right, I'll go.' Stuart grimaced in mock resignation. 'I suppose I can always get sloshed in the interval to help me through the second half.'

'Don't you dare!'

Charlotte smiled happily at him. The icy coolness with which he had greeted her on her return from London had taken some time to fade, but he had finally accepted her account of her role as the unwilling victim, and after dark talk of what he would like to do to Jude Renton if he ever got hold of him, they had both, it seemed, slipped back into their former easy relationship—for which Charlotte at least had breathed a sigh of gratitude. Working with someone as a close, daily partner was all very well, but if things went wrong between them... But nothing else is going to go wrong, she told herself stoutly. Jude's played his last trick on us. I'll make sure of that...

The early June evening was, as she had promised, fine and warm, the first real taste of summer. She bathed and shampooed her hair, then stood indecisively in front of her wardrobe. On a golden evening like this, even relatively new clothes seemed somehow dusty and tired-looking, and she had a sudden urge to seize armfuls of them, march into the garden and put a match to the lot. Somehow, nothing—her two best silk dresses, a light-weight jersey suit, even the pretty yellow poplin she had

just bought—*nothing* looked quite right, she thought
with intense dissatisfaction.

Her eyes strayed to the large plastic bag in the bottom
of the wardrobe, filled with things which she intended
to drop off at the charity shop. She rummaged through
it, among old though clean sweaters, and last winter's
two Bad Buys, then pulled out a dress and shook it from
its folds.

Of course—the very thing! Wildly unfashionable now,
for she had bought it during the last fling of the Rustic
Shepherdess look of some years before, but for tonight—perfect. An ankle-length Jane Austenish gown
of finest handkerchief-lawn, in the palest of seagreens,
the low scoop neckline and three-quarter sleeves edged
with white cotton lace, the high-waisted bodice delicately pin-tucked. She held it up in front of her and gave
an involuntary smile. Stuart had always loved her in
this—she would please him tonight by wearing it. With
luck, it would even make up for the madrigals!

The car park of the mellowed stone manor house was
almost full when they arrived and walked through into
the gardens. They were opened to visitors every summer
and Charlotte had known them since she was a child.
Now, she often brought parties of eager tourists here,
but still she never came without a lift of the spirits, a
little thrill of anticipation at seeing yet again their many
beauties.

The entertainment was to take place on the enormous
expanse of grass, bordered by high hedges, known as
the Theatre Lawn, and when she and Stuart reached it
many people were already in place. There were crowds
here, no doubt lured by a fine evening, a lovely garden,
and the pleasure—and curiosity—of seeing three well-
known actors—although not one particular very well-

known actor, as Charlotte had carefully ascertained in advance—at close quarters.

At the far end, at the foot of the shallow flight of stone steps, three cushioned wicker basket chairs had been set by a table, with a jug of water, glasses and a bowl of fat pink shrub-rosebuds. In front of them, the chairs had been arranged in loose, straggling rows forming a rough semi-circle, giving the impression of an informal, even impromptu gathering, instead of a meticulously organised event. The seats were filling up rapidly, but Charlotte and Stuart found a couple of places at the end of a row near the front and settled in them.

He opened the programme and gave a groan. 'Oh, God, look—it's endless!'

Charlotte leaned over to look at it. 'No, it isn't, Stu. I don't suppose the madrigals are very long, and most of the poems—that one, that one—oh, and the ones that Caroline Sterne is reading, they're all short, so——'

She stopped as the hum of chatter died away and a man came to the front of the stage. 'Ladies and gentlemen, if I can have your kind attention for a moment. First of all, on behalf of the organisers, may I extend a cordial welcome to you all on this glorious summer evening...'

Charlotte's eyes strayed to the hedge, and beyond to the line of mature trees and distant hills. From the fields that bordered the garden, sheep could be heard, and through the hedge came the scents of roses—or was it perhaps only her neighbour's perfume...? Beside her, she sensed Stuart give a start and her eyes returned to the man on the stage. What had he just said, to cause that murmur of subdued excitement...? 'So, while we must all commiserate with Mr Browne on his indisposition——' so Russell Browne wasn't going to be here tonight. What a pity, he'd have read that Keats ode beautifully '—we are indeed most grateful to Mr Renton for stepping in at such short notice.'

No! It wasn't true! Her ears were playing tricks. And among the group now standing in the clipped archway of the hedge, awaiting their cue, wasn't Jude—the figure must be a dreadful hallucination. But all round her a ripple of anticipation was now running through the audience, a subtle, extra thrill which was almost tangible.

'...He has most kindly waived the whole of his performing fee, his only stipulation being that a proportion of tonight's profits goes to a charity of his choosing.'

'Did you know about this?' Stuart's angry voice was in her ear.

'Of course I didn't,' she hissed. 'For goodness' sake, be reasonable, Stu! How could I possibly have known?' And if I had, she added as a silent, miserable rider, I wouldn't have come within a million miles of the place.

Stuart's reply was drowned in a surge of applause. Charlotte glanced at him and saw his set face. Oh, well, she had no time now for considering *his* finer feelings—in any case, her own were in such tumult that for a few moments she was incapable of coherent thought. Her hands, almost of their own volition, were joining in mechanically with the applause, as the three actors, followed by the madrigal group and musicians carrying an assortment of old-fashioned-looking instruments, walked out across the grass to make their bows.

She didn't want to look at Jude. Maybe, if she didn't see him, she could pretend somehow that he wasn't there. But, after all, she cared nothing for him and so, surely, she was being ridiculous. She couldn't sit for the next two hours blotting him out of her consciousness, and if

she allowed herself to be disturbed in the slightest by his
presence, a lovely evening would be ruined. He hadn't
seen her and she would just be one among a sea of
nameless faces floating in front of him. And during the
interval, he and the others would no doubt be swept off
to the manor house, so she would be quite secure.

As they bowed again in reply to the warm applause,
she at last permitted her eyes to wander along the row
until, with an unsteady flickering of her pulses that
angered her, they rested on him. This was a new Jude
Renton, a Jude she did not know, playing a role she had
never seen him in—grave, assured, an actor to the very
fingertips. Impeccably dressed—what had he said: 'My
fans expect it of me'?—in a white dinner jacket, straight
black trousers, a white frilled shirt and black bow tie,
he inclined his head in graceful acknowledgment to the
audience. Then, as his fellow actors stepped back, as
though to defer slightly to him, he abruptly sat down in
one of the basket chairs.

Charlotte stared at him, unable now to tear her eyes
from him, as she sensed dimly, for the first time, the
greatness that lay in him as an actor. There was an intensity in him tonight which she had never seen before;
although a handful of poems on a summer evening was
something he could no doubt have done off the top of
his head, using nothing but his voice and a thousandth
part of his abilities, none the less, she knew that he was
preparing himself to give as polished a performance as
for any of his most taxing stage or screen roles. Caroline
Sterne opened her book and began to read...

Gradually, under the spell of the music, songs and
poetry, Charlotte relaxed. Occasionally, when he was not
reading, she saw Jude's dark eyes wander about the
audience, and then she shrank down slightly into her

chair, but his gaze was idle, without curiosity, and the
oblique angle between them, she was sure, would render
her securely invisible. And anyway, even if he did see
her, there was nothing he could do. He was hardly likely
to leap to his feet and start hurling abuse at her in such
a public setting.

Half smiling to herself, she glanced down at the programme. It was almost the interval—just one more poem
from Jude to come. He took a few sips of water, then
launched into Marlowe's pretty lines, 'Come live with
me, and be my love.'

He paused, then laid the open book down on the table,
uncurled himself from the wicker chair, and in a silence
so profound that Charlotte was sure that her heartbeats
of sudden alarm must be perfectly audible to everyone
sitting around her, he smiled across at the lute player,
who also got up, and together they strolled across the
no-man's-land of lawn to the audience.

Jude's eyes singled out a pretty teenage girl sitting with
her parents. He stopped beside her, dropped to one knee
and, with the lute softly strumming behind him, went
on,

> 'And we will all the pleasures prove,
> That hills and valleys, dales and fields,
> Woods or steepy mountain yields.'

At the end of the verse, he straightened up, smiled at
the girl and kissed her hand, then moved on, as his ac-
companist played a haunting little melody. He did the
same with an elderly lady, leaving her as flushed and
bright-eyed as the girl had been moments before.

'Ham! Sheer ham,' muttered Stuart, and Charlotte
tried to agree. But—*somehow*, that intangible magic

which Jude carried around with him made it totally, delightfully entrancing.

Moving among the rows, he passed out of her range of vision. Other people were craning round, smiling, but Stuart was staring straight ahead and she, aware only, in every atom of her body, that somewhere behind her Jude was roaming untrammelled, was gazing at nothing at all, her hands locked together in her lap.

'And I will make thee beds of roses, And a thousand fragrant posies...' Would the poem *ever* end?

Then, simultaneously, her stomach seemed to somersault with alarm and her heart to stop beating as, from immediately behind her, Jude's voice said softly, 'A gown made of the finest wool...' and he leaned over, clasping her hand, then tightening on it as, with a great start of terror, she almost leaped out of her seat.

CHAPTER SEVEN

'No! No—please, Jude,' Charlotte managed to get out in an agonised whisper, but his hand was inexorably lifting her from her chair even as she shrank further down into it. All around her, smiling faces were turned to them, nodding in approval at the charming cameo they were no doubt making—she playing to perfection the impromptu role of the reluctant beloved of Marlowe's lines—and quite unaware of the dark undercurrents swirling around the three of them—for, as she rose reluctantly to her feet, she momentarily glimpsed Stuart's face, red with anger, as his restraining hand was swept aside.

Brilliant colour was flooding into her own cheeks, as shame and embarrassment united inside her. But what could she do, in front of two hundred people, apart, that was, from making a terrible scene? And Jude knew this, of course. Even as, for the first time, she shot him a direct, beseeching glance, she saw that he was watching her, a half-smile on his lips. He was quite clearly relishing her total discomfiture, she thought, with a despairing twist of anger. And yet, behind the smile, there was a hint of something else—secret, for her eyes alone—which made her breath quicken and which set every alarm bell in her mind ringing frantically.

The lute player was at Jude's shoulder. He was grinning, and when he caught Charlotte's eye, he winked at her encouragingly and strummed a chord. Jude was pulling her after him now, down on to the grass stage, his hands ostensibly solicitous, in reality an unbreakable grip of steel on her wrist.

He was turning her to half face the audience now. Her face hot with embarrassment still, she stood on trembling legs, her head lowered, the fingers of her free hand plucking convulsively at the ribbons of her neckline.

'The shepherd-swains shall dance and sing, For thy delights each May morning...' If only a ten-foot hole would open in front of her, so that, shamed and angry, she could jump into it. What a fool she'd been to come tonight, to play right into Jude's hands! For suddenly, with a great leap of certainty, she knew that his seemingly spontaneous walkabout had been planned from the moment he'd spotted her among the audience. His intention right from the beginning had been to trap her and——

'...If these delights thy mind may move, Then live with me and be my love.' Thank God! she thought fervently. Her torment was over. Jude bowed, acknowledging the rapturous applause, then gave her a formal half bow, and still keeping that tight hold on her, pushed her forwards a little in front of him. Charlotte ducked her head in an awkward little bow, but then, as she tried surreptitiously to move away from him, a man at the back stood up, clapping furiously and shouting, 'More, more!'

Charlotte shot him a look of pure loathing, but she was too late. Other people took up the chant, until Jude, with another half-bow and a self-deprecating gesture, silenced them. As though conscious that her shaking legs imprisoned her where she was as securely as his hand, Jude loosed his grip, and gently turned her to face him. The silence was intense; she could feel it settling all around them, something almost palpable from which she could not break free, but only stand, her breathing all but suspended.

'Shall I compare thee to a summer's day?'

There was a soft yet audible sigh from the audience as Jude began the Shakespeare love sonnet.

'Thou art more lovely and more temperate...' His voice was winding itself around her, soft as a cord of silk, caressing her, stroking her almost physically, until, against all her conscious desires, she felt herself begin to relax. Jude was willing her to look up at him—she could feel his will burning into her, and at last, in silent obedience, she shyly raised her eyes, bracing herself for the ironic mockery which she would meet. But for once there was no mockery in his expression. His eyes, very dark, were fixed on hers with an intensity which she found profoundly disturbing, and as her eyes locked with his, she felt the hectic colour fade from her cheeks, leaving her very pale.

When at last the endless fourteen lines were finished, she stood by Jude as he acknowledged the tumultuous applause, her one thought now being to escape, and at length, as the other performers gathered round and the audience began getting to their feet for the interval, Charlotte managed to give him a tight-lipped smile, not able to trust her voice, and turned away, to seek the seclusion of the long walk, the gravelled, tree-lined avenue that led from one side of the lawn.

Here she paced up and down, shivering despite the warmth of the evening, hardly aware of the buzz of talk and laughter from the far side of the hedge as she struggled for self-control. Then she stopped abruptly, with an exclamation of impatience. What on earth was wrong with her? Charlotte Mercer, a sensible, composed young woman, used to being in the public gaze every working day, reduced to trembling uncertainty by a few moments of unsought-for limelight, so that minutes later her mouth was still dry, her heart still pounding unsteadily against her dress. But it was not that, of course. She could feel, almost *see* before her—the sensation was so powerful—a gulf opening, not just between her and Stuart, but between her and everything in her safe, well-ordered life.

A group of people appeared at the far end, drinks in hand, and somehow resisting the impulse to escape further into the garden, she roused herself to return to face Stuart. But he was not on the lawn, or in the crush around the long trestle table loaded with drinks that served as a bar. Perhaps he had taken his wine and gone looking for her in the garden? She must find him, for a feeling of almost superstitious dread was beginning to pervade her, a fear that if she did not, then something terrible might happen.

He was not in the rose garden, where the scent of honeysuckle and roses hung heavy in the warm air. Charlotte went through to the ornamental pool, but although quite a crowd was there, some idly trailing their fingers through the murky water, he was not among them, so she hurried past, and down the long, winding walk that led beside the stream to the far end of the garden.

By the time she reached the ha-ha that ringed the garden, she was almost running. But Stuart was nowhere to be seen. That feeling of dread still pervading her, she turned back slowly, then caught a fleeting glimpse, at the far end of the path, of a man. Stuart! She took a few eager steps towards him, then stopped dead. It was not Stuart, but she recognised all too well the white-jacketed figure who was advancing on her with swift, purposeful strides.

She looked wildly back over her shoulder, seeking safety that way, but she had walked into a dead end. Her only escape route had been the rickety rustic bridge which crossed the stream a few yards up, and she had hesitated a fraction too long. As she reached it, Jude crossed the last couple of yards in two strides, caught hold of her by the waist and spun her round towards him.

'L-let me go!' she panted.

She backed up against the bridge in an attempt to escape, but Jude put his hands on the balustrade on either side of her, trapping her against its rough hardness.

'You should have stayed and had a glass of wine with us, as a reward.'

His voice, easy and relaxed, fuelled the anger which was rapidly taking over her fear.

'What for?' she flung at him. 'For being made a fool of by you?'

'Now would I do that, Charlotte?'

'Yes, you would. You knew how I'd feel. You—you deliberately set out to humiliate me!'

'Oh, surely not?' His voice was silky. 'You must have realised that every other woman in the audience was wildly envious of you.'

'You—you conceited, arrogant——' Charlotte broke off abruptly, then went on, 'If you did need to satisfy your over-inflated ego, why did you have to pick on me? As you say, any other woman would, no doubt, have been swooning at the feet of Jude Renton, the Great Lover——' she rushed headlong on, regardless of the warning flash of anger in his eyes '—but no, you had to indulge your own private, twisted sense of humour, setting me up deliberately to make trouble between Stuart and me.'

'Oh, and how did I do that?'

'You know very well. Bringing me out to the front, reciting those love poems. You—you were as good as m-making love to me with your voice in front of all those people!' Too late, the incautious words were out before she could prevent them.

Jude raised one eyebrow. 'And was that so terrible? Or perhaps you would prefer me to make love to you with my body, Charlotte?'

She gave a violent start as the shock of his words hit her. How could he? Whatever ruthless vendetta he was pursuing to avenge himself on her for her imagined wrongdoings, how could he be so cruel? But if he wanted to play the game that way, then somehow, for the sake of her own pride—if not self-preservation—she had to convince him that nothing he said could possibly touch her, much less hurt her.

'Good grief, no, Jude!' From somewhere, she found a scornful laugh. 'You overestimate yourself, I'm afraid. Once was plenty—more than enough, enough for a lifetime.'

Aghast at her own temerity, Charlotte braced herself for the reaction. It was very swift. Fury flared in his eyes again, and his mouth narrowed to a thin, terrifying line, but even as she, appalled by the lightning she had brought down on her own head, made a convulsive move to break out from his encircling arms, Jude tightened his grip, pinning her between them.

'No—no, Jude, I'm——' she began urgently, then froze into silence as a couple, clutching glasses of wine, appeared on the path behind them. She moved slightly, assuming that he would loose her, and preparing herself, when release came, for instant flight, but instead he came even closer to her so that, through the thin material of her dress, she could feel the taut line of his thigh against her and his warm breath stirring the strands at her hairline.

'Let me go,' she muttered in a silent, angry whisper, but he merely shook his head.

His movement had made room for the couple to pass across the narrow bridge and they did so, shooting openly curious glances at them as they went. Once they had gone on up the path, Charlotte forced herself to wait passively for him to slacken his grip, but he still made no effort to step back from her.

For an instant she gazed at him, seeing in the low rays of sunlight her own reflection staring from his eyes and feeling his heart beating against her, surely not quite steadily. Very slowly and deliberately, he bent his head towards her and, closing her eyes against the feeling of helpless suffocation that was rising within her, she swayed towards him, waiting for—— Her eyes flew wide open. What midsummer lunacy was infecting her? She jerked away from him, so that his mouth grazed her cheek.

'It—it was kind of you to step in at such short notice.' The voice was high, breathless, totally unlike her own, but she had to restore some semblance of normality to this encounter.

Jude finally drew back and looked down at her. His face was in shadow so that the expression in his eyes was masked from her.

'That poem could have been written with you in mind, you know.'

Thrown totally off balance, Charlotte could only gape at him. 'What?'

'You know—"Thou art more lovely". You really do look lovely tonight. A beautiful woman in a beautiful garden—what more could any man desire?'

He gave her a wry, slanting smile and she caught the sweetness of wine on his breath. Of course, he'd been drinking. Several glasses probably, in quick succession, before he had come stalking her through the garden. And yet surely there had been an undertone of sincerity in his voice that had not been there before and——

Charlotte glanced up quickly from under her lashes. Jude's face, his eyes looked wholly serious, she thought, with a sudden catch in her throat. She stood motionless, allowing him to put out his hand and lift a tendril of russet hair that had escaped, tucking it gently behind her ear. Then he lowered his head again and softly brushed the side of her throat with his lips while she stood as though mesmerised, helpless against the soft trembling that seemed to possess her whole body.

'Mmm.' His mouth found the telltale pulse. 'You smell gorgeous. Of summer evenings, and roses, and——'

'And *Mitsouko*,' she just managed to say through the tightness of her chest, and felt him laugh against her.

He raised his head slightly, his eyes darkening, and this time he was going to kiss her properly and she was going to surrender herself to his arms and——

From far away, a bell clanged loudly, echoing across the garden, and she heard Jude curse softly. Her eyes flew open as a cold blast of sanity returned. What folly— what utter folly had she been guilty of?

'I—I must go, Jude.'

She had to get away from this terrifying web of tension which was winding itself around her. But still he did not move.

'Please l-let me go,' she stammered. 'You'll be wanted, and I must get back.' Yes, that was it, she had to get back to Stuart.

'All right, Charlotte, no panic.'

Jude's voice sounded rough and he was breathing hard as though he had been running, but he took his hands from the bridge, lifting them in a gesture of release, and she stumbled past him. She did not know whether he was following her—she did not turn round.

At first she could not see Stuart, among all the people heading back to their seats, but then she spotted him, standing morosely by the bar, a glass in his hand. He swung round as she spoke his name.

'Where the hell have you been—or need I ask?'

Charlotte was conscious of several pairs of ears pricking up. 'Stu, please, not here,' she said in an urgent undertone. 'Let's go home—now. I-I've got a headache.'

'Suits me.'

He gulped the last of his wine, set down the glass with a thump and strode off, leaving her almost running to catch up with him. Behind her, she heard the hum of chatter die down and a burst of applause. The second half was about to begin. More than anything else, she wanted desperately just to be allowed to get home. Perhaps Stuart would relapse into one of his sulky silences and, if so, she would be intensely grateful for it. But in the deserted courtyard he stopped and caught hold of her arm.

'Just tell me this, Charlotte. What have you got going for Jude Renton?'

She stared at him, choking down a wild, almost hysterical laugh. 'W-what on earth do you mean?'

'You know quite well what I mean.' He looked at her accusingly. 'The first time I met him, at the Lunch, there was something between you two then. Don't deny it——' as she attempted to protest '—you stared at each other—oh, I don't know, as if no one else existed—as if—you were devouring each other.'

She tried to give a dismissive laugh, but the sound came out as a shaky sob. 'There's nothing between Jude Renton and me, Stu, I swear it.' Well, only anger, hatred, loathing, she thought bitterly.

She took hold of his arm in emphasis, but he shook off her hand.

'And of course I only have your word for it that that trip to London wasn't a cosy little fix between you.' As she gaped at him, he went on, 'And tonight—a right fool I must have looked, with that bastard practically undressing you with his eyes! He could hardly keep his hands off you, and you encouraging him every inch of the way!'

A gasp of outrage was torn from her. First the encounter with Jude in the garden, shaking her to the roots of her being, and now this!

'Well, if that's what you want to believe, then there's nothing more to say, is there?'

Biting her lip to keep in check the scalding tears which had sprung to her eyes, Charlotte walked off across the courtyard. Once outside on the road, though, she slowed, then finally stood irresolute. This quarrel, surely, was exactly what Jude had planned, and she and Stu were falling as neatly as apples from the bough into his manipulative hands. She almost cried out loud as this realisation hit her. He had seen her, yes, but he must also have seen who she was with. He could have left them in peace, chosen anyone—as he had boasted, any other

woman in that audience would have snatched the chance
to tell her grandchildren that Jude Renton had held her
hand while reciting a love sonnet to her.

She shook her head. How he had changed! Simon had
always been a troublemaker, a scheming though lovable
trickster. But Jude? Never. *Simon* . . . He was the key.
Jude's public humiliation of her tonight and his hunting
her down in the garden afterwards—they were both part
of his revenge, part of her punishment. 'Thou art more
lovely.' His voice echoed in her mind and for an instant
she closed her eyes, feeling again the touch of his mouth
against her soft skin . . .

Oh, Charlotte, what a fool you are! You almost fell
for it, she thought, with self-flaying contempt. He's an
actor, isn't he? OK, he looked sincere—but he's in the
business of synthetic sincerity, a changeable chameleon
who can no doubt turn on his most famous screen role,
the Great Lover, at the flick of an invisible switch, and
at no more cost to him than—than snapping his fingers.
And she, idiot that she was, had almost been taken in
down there by the stream. The tears that she had forced
back burned against her eyelids again. To Jude, it had
all been no more than a continuation of his cruel game,
while she—she stood, breath almost suspended, watching
Stuart come slowly towards her, taking out his car keys—
what did she want it to be? The answer leaped swift and
sure into her consciousness. She wanted it to be for real.
But no, that was impossible. She knew what Jude really
felt for her and nothing could ever change that. He had
deliberately, ruthlessly ruined this evening—she must not
let him ruin her—*their*—whole life.

As Stuart came up to her, she snatched hold of his
arm convulsively and buried her head in his jacket.
'Stu—please—let's get married, now. I was wrong. We

won't wait till the end of the season. Let's get a special licence.'

He held her away from him and stared at her with something, she thought involuntarily, very like alarm in his eyes.

'You're upset, Charlotte—and no wonder. You've had a hell of an evening. But no. You know we agreed to wait, and you were right about that. We're far too busy just now—and besides, we're fine as we are.'

'Yes, I suppose so.' She toyed with his lapel. 'It's— it's just that I suddenly wanted things to be different, I suppose.'

'And they will be.' Stuart smiled reassuringly at her. 'You know we've got everything worked out, and we can't spoil it all, can we? After all, it's our whole lives we're talking about, isn't it, love?'

Charlotte nodded slowly. 'Yes, you're quite right, Stu. I'm sorry.' She gave him a pale smile. 'I don't know what came over me.'

CHAPTER EIGHT

"MORNING, Stu—hi, Debbie.' Charlotte breezed into the office. 'Thank goodness for Friday!'

She hung up her bag and white linen jacket, then perched on the corner of Stuart's desk. 'You got the minibus checked all right, did you? I'd hate to think I'd got to take that group all the way to Oxford and back with that rattle under the bonnet.' She regarded him keenly. 'You did, didn't you?'

'Er—yes. It wasn't much—just a loose wire. But you needn't worry, I'm taking the trip this morning.'

Charlotte stared at him, perplexed. 'But I've got it all planned. Two colleges, the Botanical Gardens, then Blenheim and back in good time for me to get away——'

'Look, I'm sorry, love.' Stuart shook his head. 'Your weekend's off.'

'Of course it's not.'

Two spots of pink colour appeared in her cheeks. She must go. Although she was positive that, thanks to her natural resilience, she had finally recovered from the encounter with Jude, now nearly a month ago, none the less she had been feeling increasingly strained lately, and so two or three days by the sea with Jeanette, chatting over old schooldays, would give her just that short fillip she needed to get her through the rest of the season...

'I'm sorry if you've arranged something, Stu, but this weekend you'll just have to cover it yourself.'

'Well, I can't. They want you.'

'*They* want me?' she repeated, frowning. 'Who?'

'These two old ladies. They came in yesterday, after you'd left early——'

'To take those Germans to the site of the battle of Edgehill,' she reminded him tartly.

'Yes, all right,' Stuart conceded. 'But anyway they want you to go with them on a river-boat trip—just from tonight until Monday,' he added hastily, as he saw her face. 'And they've already paid in advance—money no object. I explained to them that, with it being such short notice and you having to change your plans, it would have to be double our normal rates.'

'But—but I don't like boats—you know I don't. And besides, I don't know how to drive them.'

'Oh, that's no problem.' He waved airily. 'One of them is a keen sailor, so she'll do the steering.'

Charlotte pursed up her lips. 'No, no, I'm sorry, but I'm not doing it,' she said stubbornly.

He shook his head sadly. 'Wasn't it you who thought up our motto, "We do anything"? But OK, you win. I'll ring them at their hotel, tell them it's off, and send back the money. Pity, though. One poor old thing looked as if she won't last much longer. She was telling Debbie and me how she grew up in Warwickshire sixty years ago and her dad ran one of the pleasure boats down on the river before they emigrated to Canada. It's the first time she's been back, and she wanted to show her friend the sort of boat trips she enjoyed when she was a girl.'

Charlotte looked down at the desk for a long time, seeing in her mind's eye that old lady, seventy at least, no doubt, trying for the last time to recapture those magical Edwardian afternoons of picnics, hampers and white sailor suits. She was wrong, of course, even to try; that particular magic had slipped away for ever, but still—— She cleared her throat to dislodge a painful lump and stood up.

'I'll ring Jeanette now—ask her if I can come next weekend instead.'

What had Stuart said? The boat was called the *Nereid* and she would find it moored opposite the Bancroft Gardens. Overnight case in hand, and dressed in a navy towelling white-piped tracksuit, which she had chosen with the hope that she would at least look vaguely nautical, even if she didn't feel it, Charlotte crossed the footbridge over the green depths of the River Avon and followed the path. Yes, there lay a dark blue-painted boat tied up under the willow trees: the *Nereid*. But in the evening light it looked deserted.

She leaned across and rapped tentatively at the door that led to the accommodation area. No reply. Well, the old ladies had told Stuart that they might be late, and she was to go aboard anyway. But even so, she did not feel wholly comfortable as she dumped her bags on the cramped wooden deck and swung herself over beside them.

Across the river, people were going into the Theatre for the evening performance or strolling in the gardens, still lit by warm sunshine, and all at once Charlotte felt strangely alone. She wanted to be over there, sitting on the grass, idly feeding the ducks, instead of on this silent boat. Still, she *was* here and, as a group of noisy youths came down the footpath towards her, she ducked down through the door, closing it behind her.

A largish saloon—a bedroom by night, presumably, then a small kitchen—sorry, *galley*, she corrected herself—a minute bathroom, and in the bow, another tiny cabin—hers, no doubt. She put down her case on the narrow bunk, opened one of the windows to let a current of air into the stifling cabin, then went out on deck again.

For a long time she leaned against the rail, her chin on her hands, until she saw the audience spill out on to the Theatre's riverside terrace. It must be the interval. What was tonight's play? she wondered idly, and dug out the programme from her bag, running her finger down the columns. *Coriolanus*. Oh, well, they were no doubt enjoying it—the critics had gone wild over the production, writing at great length about the sparks that flew between Coriolanus and Tullus Aufidius, but even so, *Romeo* would have been more suitable on a warm summer's evening... But when she glanced up at the sky, the sun had vanished behind a great bank of brazen yellow cloud, and she was almost sure she'd caught the distant mutter of thunder. She shivered apprehensively and glanced quickly along the bank, but no old ladies were making their purposeful way towards the *Nereid*.

Charlotte retreated to her cabin and sat up on the hard little bed, yawning with boredom and staring disconsolately out at the small patch of river bank which was visible. Where were they? If they were going to be much later, surely it would have been more sensible to make an early morning start. Oh well, no doubt they would arrive in their own good time—after all, they were paying double rates... Remembering the paperback she had tossed into her case at the last minute, she dug it out, kicked off her trainers, propped herself up near the window and turned to page one...

Her overnight bag woke her as it slipped to the floor with a dull thud. She lay bewildered for a few moments, then, as the fuzz of sleep slowly cleared, she eased herself up on one elbow. It was almost dark in the cabin now, and something surely was wrong. She sat up, her heart thumping erratically. The boat was moving, swaying slightly under her, and when she strained her ears, she could hear the faint though definite throb of the engine. She pressed her face to the glass and saw, far behind, tiny pinpricks of light—Stratford, rapidly disappearing over the horizon, a horizon lit suddenly by a flicker of white lightning. The storm was coming, but for once her fear of the elements was taking second place.

Charlotte bit her lip, furious with herself. How embarrassing! Instead of being on the deck to welcome them, she had fallen asleep, and they had been too kind to disturb her. Not stopping even to put on her trainers, she went swiftly through the other cabins, framing abject apologies en route. She quietly opened the door to the deck—then stood stock still, as though frozen into immobility. Standing at the tiller, outlined black against the still-glimmering light from the sky, was the silhouette of a man.

She gave a half gasp, half groan of shocked recognition. 'Oh God, I don't believe it!'

'Hello, Charlotte. Sorry I was late, but the performance overran a bit tonight.' Jude's voice was laconic in the extreme.

She stared at him, then, as a wild, hysterical laugh bubbled up, she clapped a hand to her mouth. She had avoided Jude assiduously for weeks, and now, through some terrible error, she was face to face with him across a yard of deck.

'Look, there must have been the most awful mix-up,' she said urgently. 'You'll have to turn around. I've got two old ladies——' She stopped abruptly, as the import of his words sank in.

'Sorry, they couldn't make it,' Jude said lightly. 'So I've come instead.'

Charlotte's knees were trembling under her, and she slid down on to the narrow, slatted bench, staring up at him in stupefied horror. Finally, she tried to speak. 'There's——' She cleared her throat of a swelling obstruction. 'There are no old ladies, are there?' she said eventually, in a flat, dead tone.

'That's right. Just two young actresses who owed me a bit of a favour and wanted to prove they could play seventy-year-olds to the manner born. They succeeded, too, didn't they?'

She could feel him smiling in the darkness, and deep inside her a small red flame of anger was fanned into life, not only for herself but for Stuart, who had been so easily conned by the duplicity of this—this—— She leapt to her feet and glared up at him, a rumble of thunder, much nearer now, cutting an even sharper edge into her voice.

'Right, well, you've had your clever little joke at our expense,' she raged, 'so now you can just turn right round.'

Jude shook his head. 'No way. Sorry, Charlotte. I've just struggled through two locks single-handed. I could have done with your help then, although I must admit,' his tone was reflective, 'the fact that you were dead to the world did, on the whole, make things considerably easier.'

So Jude was not going to take her back to Stratford! Whatever he was planning, it was more than just a silly practical joke that would soon be over. And Stuart was not expecting her back until Monday evening! As the enormity of what was happening to her began to break over her, Charlotte's stomach muscles tightened in real apprehension.

'You—you're kidnapping me!'

'Hardly the terminology I'd use. After all, I'm paying the ransom—and double rates at that.' There was an inflection in his voice which she did not care for. 'Anyway,' he went on, 'I did promise you, if you remember, that when I kidnapped you, I'd make a professional job of it.'

'Yes, but I didn't know you meant it!' she wailed, banging her fists down on the rail in impotent fury. 'Why? Why—when you hate me so much, when you bl-blame me——' she broke off, her voice quivering.

'As to the why,' Jude replied coolly, 'all will be revealed in good time.'

She stared up at him, seeing the lines of his profile, hard, implacable, against the pale sky. Jude—so unpredictable, so moody, and harbouring such contempt and hatred for her for years that he might be capable of— anything. She swallowed, her hands clenching, until she distinctly felt a nail puncture the tender skin of her palm. A scream was rising inside her and she bent her head, fighting to retain her self-control.

'Please, Jude, let me go,' she said unsteadily at last. It was what she had begged of him in the garden, but this situation which unwittingly she had been trapped into tonight was so much more threatening, dangerous. The boat gliding remorselessly over the dark water, the night closing in around them—there was a quality of nightmare about it. Perhaps in a few moments she would wake, but no, she was wide awake now.

'No, Charlotte.'

Was his tone momentarily a shade softer? Wishful thinking, no doubt. Her fingers beat a frantic tattoo on the metal rail. Beside them, a steep wooded bank was slipping past giving way to gently sloping fields. Jude edged the boat past a small area of turbulence, nearer, temporarily, to the bank, then nearer still. This might be her only chance. She threw herself at him, knocking him off balance and momentarily loosening his negligent grip on the tiller. She caught hold of it and swung it hard across towards the near bank.

For a few moments, it loomed at an alarming rate and she was bracing herself for the impact, already tensed for the wild leap to safety, when he tore her fingers away, wrenched the tiller round towards mid-river and pulled viciously on the throttle. The engine responded with a deafening roar and Charlotte was hurtled backwards against the side of the boat.

She leaned against the rail for support, nursing her smarting hands. Her leg brushed against a water can... Perhaps she could hit him on the head with it and... She was hardly conscious that she was leaning towards it, her hand outstretched, when Jude, with an exclamation of impatience, hooked it out of her reach with his foot.

'Don't try any more little tricks like that,' he said curtly. 'I might just finally run out of patience with you.'

'Well, I'll tell you something for free, Jude Renton!' she stormed at him, 'I will not stay cooped up on this boat with you until Monday, and that's a promise. You'll have to watch me every minute, and the second you turn your back, I swear I'll escape somehow. Or perhaps you're intending to tie me into my bunk. That's just the sort of behaviour I'd expect from a bully like you!'

'Don't tempt me, honey.' Jude's drawl held a grim warning which she dared not ignore.

'Well, I do hope you won't have any objections if I go to bed?' she asked, with studied, frigid politeness.

'Not at all,' he said drily. 'Have the sofa bed in the saloon if you want to.'

'How very kind of you,' she replied with heavy sarcasm, as her tongue got the better of her discretion, 'but no. As the hirer of the boat—and at double rates, I hope—you must have the best bed. As a mere kidnap victim I feel I'm much more suited to the bunk.'

Jude shrugged indifferently. 'Have it your own way.'

But I don't! she wanted to yell at him. I don't have it my way, and neither does anyone else when you're around. Instead, though, she turned and ducked through into the cabin, contenting herself with putting as much of her frustration as she dared into the slam of the door behind her.

She dragged the counterpane from the narrow bunk bed and sadistically punched the pillows into softness. As she leaned across to close the curtains, though, there was a sudden white flash of lightning, which illuminated the black, swirling water and beyond, a line of ghostly willows, and this was followed by a terrific crack of thunder. Charlotte gave a cry of real terror and, throwing herself headlong on the bed, buried her face in the pillows. She hated storms, particularly at night, but safely at home she could to an extent ignore them. Here, though—wasn't it true that lightning struck water? Supposing the next zigzag flash struck, not the water, but *them*—— She felt every muscle lock rigid with fear, and when a hand touched her shoulder, she started violently.

'Charlotte.'

'Go away.' Her voice was muffled by the pillow.

'What did you say?'

'I said go away, will you!'

She lifted her face momentarily, then flinched as the cabin was briefly illuminated again. Jude laughed softly.

'I was going to ask you whether you're still afraid of storms.'

She felt him sit on the edge of the bed and the next moment, ignoring her stifled protests, he was drawing her up to cradle her against him, his arms tight around her, his cheek against her head, soothing her in a rhythmic, stroking movement, until, unwillingly, she felt herself relax. The storm raged overhead, but for once in her life she was aware of it only on the periphery of sensation.

She lay, all her senses fully engaged by the potent nearness of Jude. His hard torso, his arms enwrapping her as though with a protective cloak, the smell of his maleness, his cheek softly rubbing against her hair... And suddenly she was filled with intense, aching longing for him, which at the same time terrified her and filled her with an exultant joy that made her want to stand on tiptoe and shout.

The storm was short and sharp. The first drops of rain changed to a deluge, then died away with a last, subdued roll of thunder. Jude held her away from him.

'All right now?'

His breath was warm against her skin but in the darkness she could only see the barest outline of his face. She rubbed her eyes, bleary from being pressed up against his shirt.

'Yes, thanks. Sorry. I-I mean——' she hesitated, embarrassed by her show of childish weakness and also, all at once, by his nearness, 'I'm all right usually these days, but it was just—the river looked so black, as if it was bottomless.'

Jude shook his head reprovingly. 'You've been watching too many late-night movies. Now,' he prodded the mattress, 'are you sure you wouldn't rather have the other bed?'

Charlotte swung her legs round to sit primly on the very edge. 'No, thank you, I'm fine here.'

That span of time, the storm, which had held them in a little bubble of intimacy, had passed, leaving her with a bewildering sense of desolation, and this put a coldness into her tone that she had not intended. Jude responded to it instantly. He straightened up as far as he was able under the low roof.

'OK, suit yourself,' he replied carelessly. In the doorway he turned back for a moment. 'See you in the morning.'

'By which time you'll have dragged me miles from home, out of reach of any chance of rescue,' she snapped, nettled by his offhandedness and sudden change of mood.

'Something like that.'

Charlotte sat staring at the door for a long time after he had gone. Just what was Jude up to this time? Why had he played this elaborate hoax? And what did he finally intend for her? Whatever it was, would she find in herself the resolution with which to combat him? Her mind strayed back to those final moments with him in the garden. Now here, once more, with his arms encircling her, she had felt a myriad conflicting emotions, tugging her in a hundred different directions. Her reason told her that she must fight against him and the feelings which he was still all too capable of arousing in her—but could she do this?

She heard the engine rev once again and felt the softly throbbing sensation that told her they were moving steadily downstream once more. There was nothing, absolutely nothing she could do until the morning. But in the meantime, she might as well lie down, although she would not allow herself to sleep, of course. She wanted to be aware all night exactly what Jude, separated from her by a couple of flimsy partition walls, was up to.

She peeled off her tracksuit, wriggled under the counterpane, and lay staring up at the roof. The gentle, regular movement and the soft slush of the river against the boat's thrust, which she could just hear, were hypnotically soothing. She felt her lids close, opened them indignantly, then felt them drift down again.

CHAPTER NINE

CHARLOTTE rolled over and came into painful contact with the side of the boat. This brought instant recollection, and she sat up stiffly, rubbing her elbow and listening for any sound. But none came, not even the faint throb of the engine; they must have stopped. She drew aside the curtain and saw that it was daylight and that they were hove to under the lee of a steep, grassy bank.

She dragged on her tracksuit and, without bothering even to pull a comb through her sleep-tangled hair, went quickly through the boat. But Jude was not there, nor outside on the deck, and when she hesitantly knocked at the tiny bathroom compartment the door swung open to reveal that it was empty.

Without stopping to consider an instant longer, she snatched up her shoulder bag and case and almost sprinted out on to the deck again. No doubt she was miles from Stratford, but somehow, if she had to crawl home on her hands and knees, she would escape. Set in the bank were some flat stones which served as rough steps. She threw her gear over the side, jumped out, then, breathless with terror, scrambled up to the top of the bank—where she came face to face with Jude.

'Going somewhere, Charlotte?' With one swift glance, he took in her and her case. 'I'll take that.' He prised it from her fingers one by one and transferred it to his own hand.

'That's mine. Give it to me. I'm leaving, and what's more, I intend to report you to the police.'

Charlotte made a snatch for her case, but he held it out of reach.

'And just what do you propose telling them?' There was the faintest undercurrent of lazy amusement in his voice.

'Oh, false pretences, detaining me against my will, grievous bodily harm—don't you worry, I'll make it sound good.'

Jude shook his head reflectively. 'I wonder who they'll believe, you or me? On balance me, I think.'

Suspicion darkened her eyes. 'What do you mean? You needn't think you're going to intimidate me any longer, Jude Renton! If I tell the truth, there'll be——'

'Oh, dear!' His voice throbbed with a sorrow which could almost have brought tears to her eyes. 'And I was hoping you wouldn't force me to reveal the unedifying truth. How, when I got back to the boat last night, I found a young lady tucked up in my bunk—naked, I should think. Yes, that sounds good. And panting for me to give the performance of my life. Occupational hazard, I'm afraid.' He spread his hands regretfully. 'Need I go on?'

'No, don't bother.' Sick at heart, Charlotte said dully, 'You win—I can't go to the police, but you can't keep me on the boat. I'm going now, with or without my bag, and if I have to walk all the way home——'

'Of course,' he interrupted her, ruminatively, 'I could always tell Fletcher roughly the same story. I don't imagine he'd be very pleased to think that you and I had cooked up those two dear old ladies to keep him happy while we skipped off together for a stolen weekend.'

Charlotte favoured him with a long look of intense loathing, then thrust her hands deep into her pockets, as the surging, primitive urge to leap at him, tear him apart, became almost too much for her to contain. She wanted to tell him to go to hell and take his boat with him, but she dared not indulge herself with that luxury. She knew that Jude was fully prepared to carry out his threat and, at best, Stuart would be terribly angry, while at worst he would be badly hurt, and she could not have that... There was nothing for it. She would have to go along with Jude's autocratic plans—whatever they were—hoping only that he would return her on Monday so that Stu would be none the wiser. She scuffed one trainer round and round in the dust, then,

'All right, Jude, you win—absolutely.' Her voice was flat. 'But you knew that already, of course. You know that I care far too much for Stuart to risk him being upset.'

She looked up at him, steeling herself to meet the inevitable contempt, but instead there was a fleeting spark of anger in those blue-black eyes—anger, and something else even more transient, which she could not recognise. He put his hand on her arm, but she tried to shake it off.

'Don't worry, I know the way.'

She turned back towards her floating prison, but Jude shifted his grip to her wrist and to her astonishment turned away from the river. Along the top of the bank where she had fought and lost the battle was an overgrown hawthorn hedge, and she saw, set in it, a wicket gate. Jude pushed it open with his foot and urged her, none too gently, past him on to a paved path. It led, she saw with amazement, to a small black and white timbered cottage whose existence had been totally unsuspected from the river, for the hedge extended round it on all four sides, enclosing it in a private world of its own. In front of the cottage was a square paved terrace, with a patio table and chairs, sun-loungers, and beyond was a pretty, though unkempt flower garden.

But Jude gave her no time to stand and admire. He walked her swiftly down the path, as though impelled by an urgency which she could not begin to comprehend, to the front door. Putting his hand on the latch, he casually opened it, but when he motioned her inside she hung back. The cottage must belong to friends of his; even Jude, she thought, would not stoop *quite* to breaking and entering, but she herself felt a sudden overpowering reluctance to enter, until he gave her a smart shove so that she stumbled forwards into the kitchen.

There was no one there. Only, she took in with a rapid, all-encompassing glance, the remains of a meal—from at least the previous day, she suspected—and a sink unit piled high with dirty dishes. No woman would have tolerated a kitchen like this for an hour. The cottage must belong to a——

Her eyes swivelled back to Jude and found him watching her. He shot her a malicious smile. 'That's right—got it in one. It's mine. At least, I've rented it—and the *Nereid*—for the season. It's my bolt-hole.'

'And you intended to bring me here all the time, didn't you? All that *charade*,' Charlotte almost spat out the word, 'about the boat was a stupid game?'

'Not a game, no.'

'But—but why?' She was so bewildered that she was almost forgetting to be angry.

Jude dumped her case on the pine table in the centre of the room. 'Necessary deception,' he said succinctly.

'If I'd come into that office of yours and said, "Charlotte, I want you to spend a long weekend with me at my secluded riverside cottage, all modern amenities and far from prying eyes", would you have leapt up and down in unrestrained joy?'

'No,' she replied briefly.

'That's what I suspected,' he said drily. 'So, hence the deception. The old Charlotte would never have been able to resist a sob story—I calculated right, it seems. Although I think the way your boyfriend's——' he somehow managed to make an insult out of the word '—eyes lit up, from all accounts, at the prospect of renting you out for the weekend——' there was a sneer in his voice and Charlotte crimsoned with mortified misery '—he would have been quite prepared to sell you to me, body and soul, for a few pounds more. So, as I've paid very handsomely for your services, perhaps you would desist from looking at me as though deciding where exactly to plunge in the carving knife.'

She stared at him, trying in vain to banish the terrifying thought that had sprung fully grown into her mind at his words.

'But—but what is it you want of me?' she got out at last, and backed up against the sink for support.

'Oh, don't worry, nothing—sinister.'

Again, there was no hint of humour in his smile, as he stood with his arms folded, watching her narrow-eyed, as though to gauge her reactions.

'*Antony and Cleopatra* opens in less than two weeks and the whole thing's crumbling about our ears. A couple of days ago our dear Cleo,' his voice was ironic, 'snapped a tendon, so she's out of action for months. Good riddance as far as I'm concerned. The only part she's a natural for is the Shrew.'

'Are you getting a replacement for her?'

'Yes,' he replied briefly. 'But that's not what's really bugging me.' His voice was taut. 'My problem is my bloody lines. I'm so used to filming these days, one scene at a time endlessly, and the cues—even my lines, if necessary—in front of me, and now they will not stick.' He struck his forehead in angry frustration.

'But you never had that problem in—in the old days. And,' Charlotte hurried on, 'you've been all right in *Coriolanus*.'

'Yes, but Aufidius is quite a small role—a good role, but he's not got that many lines. Antony's different. That's the big one. I wanted to play the part—I've come here to play the part, and now——' Jude broke off, his lips tightening '—I'm beginning to think the whole idea of coming back to Stratford was a monumental mistake.'

Their eyes met and Charlotte saw fleetingly in his a pain which, some instinct told her, was not in the least to do with failure to learn his lines. Unthinkingly, she put her hand on his arm, but he drew away as though the touch had burned him and, rebuffed, she thrust her hands in her pockets as he went on harshly,

'And so, my dear Charlotte, this is where you come in. I'm off until the Monday evening performance of *Coriolanus* and by then I intend to be word-perfect. I want no interruption of any description while I work. I've hired your services and you will look after me, starting with clearing up this disgusting mess,' he gestured towards the sink, 'cooking, and when necessary hearing my lines. Is that quite clear?'

She gazed at him speechless, but behind her blank expression, her mind was racing in overdrive. Three days. Well, three days was only—three days, after all. No, it wasn't. Cooped up in this cottage in enforced intimacy with Jude, having to dance meekly to any tune he chose to call—that spelled Endless. Waves of raw panic rose inside her. She simply could not do it. He must see that. A thought floated into her mind and she snatched eagerly at it.

'Those two actresses—surely one of them would do it?—just as a favour, of course.' She couldn't resist the dig.

'No.' Jude shook his head decidedly. 'I'm not prepared to involve any of the company in this. You'll do admirably, I'm sure.' She looked at him and saw that the steely hardness of his tone had extended to his eyes. 'Or do I have to remind you of Stuart, blissfully unaware of your present whereabouts?'

She scanned his face for any sign of softening towards her, but there was no mercy in those eyes.

'No.' The reply was almost torn from her. 'You don't have to remind me. You've made our respective positions quite clear. I would just like to point out that, purely in my opinion, of course, you are a rat of the first order. A tyrannical rat,' she added as an afterthought, then turned away to the sink. 'And now, oh, gracious lord,' she said over her shoulder, with a frisson of fear at her own daring, 'perhaps you will allow your humble and obedient slave to wash up?'

'That can wait. I'll show you your room now, then I can get to work.'

Charlotte had, a moment before, made a private resolution to guard her tongue, but this was too good an opportunity to miss. 'Oh goody, I'm to have a real room, am I?' she said in a tone of sugary sweetness. 'I thought that as a mere body slave, I might, if I was lucky, be allowed to share the dog kennel.'

Jude gave an abrupt laugh. 'Apart from the fact that I don't keep a dog, you've got your vocabulary all wrong, sweetheart. A house slave is what you mean. A *body* slave is something altogether different. In that—er—position, you'd be in my bed, not my non-existent dog kennel, and even your beloved Stuart might baulk at that.'

He picked up her bag and disappeared up a flight of narrow stairs which led directly out of the kitchen, leaving her acutely aware that she had had the worst of that verbal exchange. When she followed, she found him waiting impatiently on the small galleried landing, which would, she supposed, have been the children's bedroom years before. There were just two doors.

'My bedroom and,' Jude gestured across the landing, 'the bathroom. You're in the attic.'

So it was to be the servants' quarters, after all. A folding metal ladder-staircase led up through an open trapdoor, and Jude gestured her ahead of him. Once in the room, though, her vision of the rusty iron bedstead, the cheerless grate and mind-improving tracts faded abruptly. At the far end of the long room the roof line came down steeply into dormers, with a slanting window set between them, but the near end had been turned into a simple bedroom. The single divan was covered with a patchwork quilt, there was an old-fashioned pine dresser, and the stained floorboards were covered with Indian rugs in bright colours.

Charlotte crossed over to the window, ducking under the sloping ceiling, and pushed it open. Directly below her, on the wall, were the topmost branches of an old, gnarled pear tree, the shoals of tiny green fruit already forming among the leaves, while beyond the hedge she

had a clear view of a long curve of the river. A group
of magpies flapped clumsily across the nearest field.

'One for sorrow, two for joy.' She was not aware that
she had murmured the old rhyme aloud, until Jude said
just behind her,

'Seven of them altogether. What's that?'

She hesitated a fraction too long, then blurted out,
'It's—it's "seven for a secret that may not be told".'

'And have you got one? A secret that may not be told?'
His voice was insistent.

Her tensed hands were gripping the window sill, but
somehow she managed to shrug carelessly, 'Hasn't
everyone?'

She pushed past him, went over to the bed and tossed
her shoulder bag down, but it fell awkwardly and the
catch burst open under the impact, spewing the bulging
contents across the width of the counterpane. With an
exclamation of irritation, she plumped down and began
cramming everything back in, anyhow.

As she refastened the clasp, Jude put her overnight
case down on the bedside rug. From the corner of her
eye, she saw him stiffen and dart a swift glance at her,
then stoop to retrieve something. He straightened up
slowly, gazing down at the photograph in his hand, and
at the mere sight of it, her insides lurched with shock.

She held out a slightly unsteady hand. 'Can I have it,
please?'

But he ignored her and stood very still, staring at it
as though she had ceased to exist. How often, she told
herself wretchedly, had she, catching sight of the photograph as she delved through her bag for something else,
called herself all kinds of sentimental fool for being weak
enough to keep it with her at all times, instead of
throwing it into a drawer, to be forgotten—or better still,

burning it. But no, in her bag it had to remain—until now.

Tentatively, she put out her hand again, risking a quick glance up at him. She had feared to meet his look, but she saw that his face was perfectly expressionless. Whatever fleeting, wrenching emotions he had experienced at seeing the three of them, caught timelessly in that happy, gilded final summer, she leaning against him, one hand resting on Simon's shoulder as he sprawled against her knees, he had subdued them.

But instead of handing it back to her, his fingers closed on it more tightly. Just for a moment, the naked, destructive pain inside him was there, so that she wanted to jump up, cradle him in her arms, and say, 'Jude, let's end this silent hating, let's talk about those days when we were all three so happy. Let's talk about Simon.' But already his face had become again that of the bleak stranger she had encountered at the Birthday Lunch, so all she said was, 'Please, can I have it back?'

Without looking at her, he thrust it into his pocket and turned towards the door. 'Eventually.'

However much he might have schooled his expression, though, there was a ragged undertone to his voice that betrayed him, she thought. But, as though to re-emphasise their positions, he turned in the doorway, 'Don't be long. I want my breakfast.'

There was a challenge behind the words, but, contenting herself with one smouldering look, Charlotte unzipped her case with a vicious jerk of the thumb and began pulling out her clothes.

'I'm going to unpack first,' she said defiantly, 'then shower and change.'

Jude eyed her thoughtfully across the width of the room, then ostentatiously looked at his watch. 'I'll give you fifteen minutes,' and he was gone.

CHAPTER TEN

CHARLOTTE resisted the frustrated, angry impulse to tear the door open and scream abuse at his back. Instead, she tugged off her trainers and began calmly, methodically hanging up her clothes in the wardrobe.

It was going to be a hot day; her tracksuit was already sticking uncomfortably to her back. She looked out clean underwear, the white halter-neck top and brief yellow denim shorts in which she had been hoping to sunbathe on the deck, while those non-existent old ladies lapped up the green watermeadows of Warwickshire. Discarding the tracksuit, she wrapped herself with extreme care in her full-length flowery cotton housecoat, and, clutching her clothes and spongebag, descended gingerly to the bathroom.

She toyed briefly with the idea of a deliberately leisurely bath, but the thought of Jude, pacing bad-temperedly below while he awaited his breakfast, was in the end too unnerving, so she contented herself, after a struggle with the controls, with a shower. She dressed quickly, then rubbed a film of moisturiser over her skin. Her hair was heavy against her neck and she could feel beads of sweat on her nape, so she dug out two white towelling bandeaux and fixed a fat bunch of hair over each ear. Well, at least she would be cool, if not elegant.

Gathering up her things, she opened the door—just as Jude came out of his bedroom opposite. It was as neatly done as a French farce, she thought wildly, but the spark of amusement died as she took in that he too had changed, from the pale grey cords, matching jacket and white shirt that he had been wearing, to a navy towelling robe, casually belted to leave most of his tanned chest and legs bare. It needed little imagination for her to realise that under it he was naked... The colour flooding into her cheeks, she swivelled her eyes quickly to his face as he looked at his watch.

'At last—half an hour.'

Charlotte had just about recovered sufficiently to reply, 'I-I couldn't get the shower to work properly.'

Jude clicked his tongue in mock sympathy and said solicitously, 'Oh, I'm sorry. You should have called me.'

Refusing to rise to the bait in his tone, she moved towards the attic staircase and he called after her, 'And by the way, I've had my breakfast. I got tired of waiting.'

She paused half-way up the steps. 'I'm so sorry.' Then, just as the bathroom door was closing, she added for good measure, 'I must make a note of that—one meal not prepared. Remind us to make you a refund for that.'

There was cereal, bread and a toaster out on the kitchen table. The combination of her ill-temper and constant apprehension over Jude's proximity had combined to destroy totally a normally healthy appetite, but she forced herself to tip a dozen or so cornflakes into a bowl and distribute milk over them individually.

She was in the middle of washing up when behind her she heard him come into the kitchen. She risked a sideways glance and saw that he had shaved and discarded the robe for faded, hacked-off denim shorts. They moulded to his flat abdomen, the curve of his thighs. That powerful, beautiful body...

'Now what's the matter?'

Jude's voice startled her. She had not realised that he was watching her, and she turned back hastily to the dirty saucepan she had been wrestling with.

'If you must know,' she said frostily, 'I was just wondering how come a rich man like you can't afford a decent pair of shorts—or at least some scissors to trim off all that fray.'

He gave a snort of laughter. 'Sorry if my shorts offend your immaculate standards, but when you spend most of your time climbing in and out of one heavy costume after another—well, an outfit like this, believe me, is quite a relief. But if it bothers you, and you're a good girl, Charlotte,' she could hear the laugh in his voice and set her teeth, 'you shall trim them off for me, give them impeccable hems. Although,' his voice changed to reflective, 'not, I think, with me in them. I don't fancy letting you loose near me with a pair of scissors in your hand!'

She banged down the saucepan into the rack so that it bounced. 'Didn't you say you'd got work to do?'

'So I have.' But he made no move to leave. 'Oh, and by the way, just wash these through for me while you've got your hands in water.'

Charlotte looked round as he tossed a pile of crumpled shirts down on to the table, then stared at him speechless. She had, just one second before, been telling herself that, like it or hate it—and she hated it—the invidious position which he had schemed her into, forced her to accept her humiliation. There was nothing she could do—at least, temporarily. When she was safely back in Stratford, Stuart still happily in ignorance, then she might allow herself the luxury of lying awake nights happily plotting how to upend Jude head over heels over Clopton Bridge one moonless night. But now—pride, if nothing else, demanded that a client of Anything Goes had his money's worth.

All this had just flitted through her mind. She seized another saucepan and began savaging it with the pan scrubber. He would not win. She would remain coldly, aloofly dignified, throughout this whole appalling weekend.

'Did you hear what I said?'

Out of the corner of her eye, she saw him move a shade closer.

'Yes.' She dragged the scrubber over the encrusted base of the pan. 'Can't you afford a washing-machine?' In spite of her tremor, the words were already off her lips.

'It packed up a few days ago, and as you were coming, well——' Jude gave a little shrug '—I didn't bother.'

Momentarily, her busy fingers stilled. So it had been no casual, last-minute, spur-of-the-moment decision to ensnare her. But she would still not give him the satisfaction of reacting. Instead, she shot him a swift look, surprising a glint of sardonic amusement.

'You said something?' He raised his dark brows interrogatively.

'Not a word.'

'Right. I'll call you when I want you,' he said off-handedly, and sauntered out.

When she was quite sure that he was gone, Charlotte dropped the saucepan and stood staring out across the small patch of garden to the hedge that marked the boundary of her prison. 'Stone walls do not a prison make, nor iron bars a cage.' No, but tall hawthorn hedges did. It was not going to be the work that would get her down over the next three days—she had never been frightened of hard work. No—she knew it now—it was the constant nearness of Jude which would make her captivity unbearable. She had thought he would have changed during the years of his absence, but under the skin of the suave, internationally successful actor he was still exactly the same: the mercurial, wholly unpredictable temperament, the dark, sombre moods instantly changed to light, then back again. A few minutes ago, the old, teasing Jude had for brief seconds looked out at her from the hostile stranger's face before the shutter descended once more.

'Have you got one—a secret that may not be told?' Suddenly, and quite beyond her control, the past was rising before her, familiar—achingly familiar—yet menacing, and spiralling coils of panic writhed in her stomach. How could she possibly hope that the next three days would pass without those memories—those accusations of her casual fickleness—surfacing once more, and when they did, how could she answer them? If she denied them, told Jude the truth, told him the secret she had kept from him for seven years—she trembled to contemplate how he might react.

Keep calm, she told herself, you must keep calm—and the panic retreated just a little way away from her. Work, keeping Jude at a distance and her mind busy, that would be her salvation. She bent over the washing-up bowl again, and when she had finished, she washed the heap of shirts and pegged them out on the line behind the cottage. Jude, she saw with relief, when she took a quick peep round the corner, was settled on the patio on one of the sun-loungers, reading with a cassette tape recorder beside him.

The french windows to what was obviously the sitting-room stood open, so Charlotte went in. It was a pleasant enough room, the furniture comfortable-looking, but although very different from the London service apartment, yet it gave her the same sensation. For all his money, she thought sadly, Jude led a totally rootless existence. True, he had that white-pillared mansion far away in California, but otherwise, nothing. How different from his childhood at the Manor, with the security of a close-knit, loving family... She angrily pushed away the sentimental thoughts. What a marshmallow fool she was turning into! If Jude lived this nomadic life most of the time, well, it must be because he chose to—there could be no other reason.

There was one thing in the room, though, that she knew instinctively belonged to him, and not simply because it did not fit with the rest of the characterless furnishing. It was a large picture, hanging on the wall opposite the window as though to catch the full light. At first, it seemed merely a glorious surreal sunburst of yellow and burning orange, but as she studied it more closely the picture took shape. It was of a giant bird, a huge phoenix, blazing with heat. The artist had caught the moment when the bird, just risen from the ashes of its old self and with the flames still flickering around it, was raising its beaked head proudly, joyously flexing its outspread wings in the ecstasy of being alive once more...

All at once, the painting was setting up within her a turbulence of conflicting emotions which she could not understand, and she was glad to turn away from it. The room badly needed cleaning, and she set to work with carpet sweeper, duster and can of polish. She had finished and was just picking a bunch of the big yellow daisies that grew in clumps outside the french windows and, Jude out of sight round the corner, temporarily forgotten, she was even humming to herself, when she heard a peremptory call,

'Hey, Charlotte, come here!'

'There's no need to yell. I can hear you perfectly well,' she said frigidly.

He watched her walk towards him, her hands full of the yellow flowers, and raised his eyebrows ironically. 'Beautifying my bachelor pad, I see. When you can tear yourself away from horticulture, I want some coffee.'

'Please,' she said sweetly. 'I want some coffee, *please*.'

He gave her a look over the top of his sunglasses, as though she were some kind of alien species, then, 'Get me some coffee,' there was a pause, 'please.'

When she returned with the mug, she held it out to him, but not taking his eyes from the book in front of him, he gestured impatiently for her to put it on the ground. She set it down, then stood in front of him. He was engrossed in a tape recording which was running softly, but finally he raised his head, his eyes invisible behind the lenses.

'Well?' Irritation, which he made no effort to control, was crackling in his voice, and he leaned over to click off the cassette.

'I was wondering,' Charlotte said hesistantly. 'What do you want for lunch?'

'Oh, for crying out——!' Jude compressed his lips angrily. 'Anything. Anything will do.' And she retreated hastily as he switched on the tape again.

It was far too hot to stay indoors, so she spent the rest of the morning assiduously weeding the flowerbeds at the far side of the cottage. At last she straightened up, easing her back, and glanced at her watch. Heavens, was that the time? She tiptoed to the corner and peeped round. Jude was still intent on his lines; she heard the soft rise and fall of his voice, then an impatient exclamation as, presumably, he faltered. Oh well, perhaps lunch would sweeten him up a fraction.

In the kitchen, Charlotte anxiously surveyed the varied contents of the fridge. Not daring to risk exposing to Jude's caustic tongue anything ambitious, she opted for scrambled eggs, one of the few dishes that she could usually rely on to turn out properly. Half a dozen eggs, a good spoonful of cream, black pepper. She set a tray neatly, then piled the creamy concoction on to toast and carried it out.

As she crossed the patio to him, Jude dropped his book and stretched luxuriously. 'About time—I'm starving! What is it?'

'Scrambled egg,' she replied, in a neutral tone. She had made that decision that, come hell or high water, he would not succeed in riling her, and he would not.

He took off his sunglasses and scowled up at her. 'Scrambled egg?'

Charlotte took a deep breath. 'You said anything would do,' she pointed out, with controlled reasonableness.

'Well, I don't fancy scrambled egg,' he said, in a tone of finality. 'You'll have to do something else.'

Charlotte, the nervous tension bubbling up inside her again, stared thoughtfully down at him for long moments as, with the weary air of a man tried beyond all human endurance, he leaned forward to pick up his book again. Then, very slowly and deliberately, she took the plate off the tray, threw the tray down on the grass, lined Jude up very carefully in her sights and carefully tipped the plate so that all the scrambled egg cascaded gently down over him.

By the time Jude, uttering a short, sharp obscenity, had leapt to his feet, scattering debris, the hysterical laugh which had welled up inside her had died away and sheer panic had replaced the momentary jubilation that had accompanied her rash act.

'What the bloody hell did you do that for?' he shouted furiously at her.

Inwardly she quaked, but somehow she returned his ferocious scowl. 'Because y-you're—you're an ill-mannered pig,' she stammered, torn between anger and terror.

The terror won, as Jude, that warning flush on his face and obviously beside himself with rage, reached out to seize her. She hesitated one moment longer, trying to stand her ground fearlessly, but then, too late, turned to flee towards the cottage. He grabbed her round the waist and dragged her, kicking and struggling, down with him on to the grass, totally indifferent to her wild shouts and flailing arms. Maddened and humiliated, she twisted her head, trapped against his knee, and sank her teeth hard into the tender flesh of his inner thigh. The effect was instantaneous though hardly gratifying. Jude swore again and pushed so that she rolled away. One of her bandeaux had come adrift; she brushed the tangle of hair from her face and sat up rather shakily.

He was examining his leg, where she could see a horribly distinct set of teeth marks, a trickle of blood oozing from several.

'I-I'm sorry,' she whispered, shocked almost into silence, 'but you shouldn't have done it.'

'You're very fortunate I haven't really set about you.' Jude still sounded furious and he shot her a grim smile. 'As it is, I'd better go and bathe these vixen fang marks before I get tetanus at the very least!'

When he had gone, Charlotte sat hugging her knees and gently rocking to and fro in silent misery. Violent tremors were running through her whole body, as though she had ague. What was happening to her? she thought, panic-stricken. In the space of a few hours, she had slipped from being a civilised, well-behaved adult into a violent, aggressive urchin—in fact, she was rapidly reverting to the seven-year-old who had, in a fit of temper, thumped Jude with his own bicycle pump when he refused to play french cricket with her, only to be upended by him and given the thrashing of her young life, so that her bottom had tingled for days. When she had complained to Gran, she had merely sniffed and remarked, 'Hmm, just be grateful if he never gives you worse, you aggravating little madam!' Prophetic words... Overwhelmed by misery and pain, Charlotte laid her cheek against her knees and closed her eyes, as a huge tear trickled down her face.

She did not hear Jude returning. A leg brushed against her head and she went rigid, then, before she could move, he plumped down beside her and put an arm roughly round her shoulders, pulling her towards him. She turned her wet face to his chest as he whispered against her hair, 'Shh! I'm sorry if I hurt you, but don't cry, Charley, please.'

Charley. At the old, childish name she gave a choked wail and abandoned herself wholeheartedly to unrestrained sobs. Jude shook her gently. 'Stop it, you'll drown us both!'

She felt him reach into his shorts pocket and then he was turning her face up, mopping at it with his handkerchief. She struggled for composure and the sobs died away into a watery snuffle. Then, without meeting his eyes, she took the handkerchief and wiped away the last few tears.

As she handed it back, she caught sight of the bite, inflamed and angry. She looked at him, her eyes blurring, afraid of his quite justifiable anger, but instead, his gaze held an expression half indulgent, half humorous, which shattered her new-found fragile composure more neatly than even his anger had done. Charlotte bit her lip on an agonised, guilty sob and the corners of her mouth turned down.

'I'm sorry, Jude. I shouldn't have done it. I d-don't know what came over me.'

He gave her a rueful smile. 'I guess we both had a temporary aberration. I must be more overwrought about *Antony* than I realised. I forgot——' His eyes left her face and travelled slowly down over her throat and the curve of her breasts, taking in, she knew, the quick, flurried breathing. His lips tightened and he uncoiled himself, pulling her up with him in one fluid movement. '—I forgot, Charlotte, that you're a grown-up young woman and much too old to chastise,' he went on tightly. 'Now, let's go in and make some cold meat sandwiches and salad.'

He rested his arm, almost as though without thinking, across her shoulders for a few moments once more, then dropped it hastily, as if her bare skin had scorched him. The deliberate gesture and the equally deliberate use of her full name pained her, though she understood. Of course—he already repented of the tenderness he had just shown and was now saying, OK, I was wrong to attack you, but the apology's over—nothing has changed.

And he was right. The abyss of memory that stretched like a black gash between them was too real, too deep ever to be bridged. She would stay securely on her side, while Jude would stay on his. It was much the best way—

the only way, in fact. If either of them took so much as a step, they would both be plunged into dark, immeasurable depths, which could destroy them both.

CHAPTER ELEVEN

JUDE was almost silent while they ate at the kitchen table, as though throwing a smokescreen of reserve around him, and his face wore that same look which even as a teasing child she had feared—an aloof, withdrawn expression that had always held her more successfully at arm's length than any snarl would have done. The moment they had finished, he pushed back his chair.

'Come on. No, leave that,' as she began to clear away, 'I want you to help me with my lines.'

Charlotte followed him back out to the patio, reminding herself that, after all, this was why she was here, but the prospect of an interminable afternoon spent with Jude and his lines somehow managed to be thoroughly demoralising. He dragged over another garden lounger and placed it carefully opposite him. Charlotte surreptitiously edged it a few inches further away with her foot and sat down as he tossed a well-thumbed copy of *Antony and Cleopatra* into her lap.

'We'll start where I left off—Act Four, Scene Twelve. Got it?' He glanced at her. 'What's the matter?' There was a touch of impatience in his voice and she began hastily flicking through the dog-eared pages.

'Nothing—nothing at all.' After all, she could not possibly tell him that she felt a shy reluctance to see him at work, preparing for a role.

He gave her a sharp look but only said, 'Right..."Yet they're not join'd: where"——' he frowned '—"where yond pine does stand, I shall discover all: I'll bring thee word straight how 'tis like to go.''' There was a short silence. 'Well, cue me back in, for God's sake!'

His fingers tapped impatiently against the side of the lounger and Charlotte frantically skimmed down the lines, then said, '"Of what he has and has not".'

"'All is lost! This foul Egyptian hath betrayed me..."'

The magic of his voice flowed over her and she let her attention stray past the page to Jude. He was leaning back, his eyes closed, frowning in concentration, and she studied him furtively, aware of the danger yet unable to drag her gaze from him. Even like this, in old denim shorts, a faded drill sunhat, his long, powerful body sprawled negligently on the lounger, one knee up so that the sun glinted on the sheen of dark hairs, there was a subtle something—she supposed it was that elusive element called star quality. Under the shadow of the disreputable hat, his thick hair looked so black that it seemed to have a bluish glint on it like a raven's wing. His mouth, sensitive but firmly etched, with a hint of the cruelty which could lurk—her own mouth tightened for an instant—yet with that hint of erotic sensuality that drove his female fans almost wild...

Without warning, phrases from that magazine article resurfaced in her mind: '...Behind the genuine charm lurks something dark, dangerous, even deadly that women find both terrifying yet sexually irresistible... That hint of menace in those brooding, brilliant eyes...'

Charlotte raised her own and realised with a start that they were fixed on her. In the shadow cast by the brim of his hat their expression was quite unreadable, but she jumped like a nervous cat.

'When you're quite ready.' Was there a faint irony?

'Sorry. I-I seem to have lost my place,' she babbled.

'Yes, you have, haven't you?' The irony was unmistakable now, and she turned quickly back to the book on her lap, blushing with confusion.

Somehow they lurched through the act towards Antony's death, Jude, increasingly irritable, working them both unmercifully in the broiling afternoon heat, and Charlotte screwed up already with her own nervousness, catching as well the tension she sensed in him...

At last he was beginning Antony's suicide speech. '"Thrice nobler than myself! Thou teachest me..."' He seemed to have forgotten that this was a mere practice. His voice, filled with anguish, lapped itself around her, moving her to an empty desolation far beyond tears, so that, almost unnoticed, her book dropped. '"...I will be a bridegroom in my death, and run into't as to a lover's bed. Come, then——"'

She was still staring at him spellbound when he looked directly across at her. 'Well? Come on.' His voice was jagged-edged with frustration.

'Oh, sorry.' Charlotte fumbled blindly through the book.

'For heaven's sake, Charlotte!' Jude exclaimed furiously, and hurled his copy at her, but she, still entranced by the seductive power of his voice, stared speechlessly at him, her eyes filling.

His mouth tightened and he leaned across, brushing away a tear that hovered on her lashes. Just for an instant his fingers touched her cheek, then he jackknifed upright and, pulling off his hat, ran his hands impatiently through his hair.

'Oh, God, I've had it for today.' He pulled a wry face. 'And as the sun sinks slowly in the west, we bid farewell, noble Antony!'

Charlotte glanced at the hands of her watch and
gasped with astonishment. They had been working out
here for hours, and when she moved she felt stiff all
over, bruised by Jude's intellectual assault and the
struggle to keep up with him. She straightened up slowly
and eased her aching shoulders, feeling rather like a
sponge which had been wrung out until it squeaked, then,
momentarily dizzy, she put her hand to her head and
collapsed back again. Jude squatted on his haunches
beside her and tilted her face up towards him.

'You look pale.'

'Oh, I'm all right. I must get you something to eat.'

She struggled to get up, brushing her hair back from
her damp forehead, but he pushed her gently down again.

'You stay right there. I've worked you like a brute all
afternoon, so the least I can do is get a meal. And
anyway, I don't want to risk scrambled egg again.'

He flashed her a warm grin which made her insides
seem fluttery, as though they were filled with feathers,
then silenced her feeble protests with a finger across her
lips. Jude gently brushed it along the soft outline of her
mouth, then, as their eyes met, his hand stilled.

'Charlotte——' he began, his voice husky. Then, as
she still looked up at him, he drew back, abruptly lifting
his finger from her mouth, and straightened up, leaving
the blood singing in her ears. 'Will a steak and salad
suit you?'

She was intensely grateful for his return to brusque
normality; it enabled her somehow at least to make the
attempt to subdue her own turmoil of emotions. 'Y-yes,
that'll be fine, thank you.'

Her own voice was stilted, but with only the faintest
tremor of unsteadiness, and when he had disappeared
into the house she got up and wandered aimlessly round

the garden. She hugged her arms to her as she stopped to watch a sparrow in the hedge, bent to sniff at a rose, yet all the time, as though she were being tossed on some dark, fathomless sea, the bewilderment was churning inside her. This peculiar feeling of disorientation—surely it could not be the result of Jude's simple gesture, his finger across her lips? The back of her neck felt hot and when she glanced down at her shoulders and arms, her normally pale skin was flushed deep pink. She had had too much sun; yes, that was it, that was all that was wrong with her... And yet that strange, disembodied feeling would not go away...

When, after she had finished washing up, she looked in at the sitting-room, she saw Jude, stretched full-length on the sofa, his hands linked behind his head, his eyes closed and a pained expression on his face as he listened to a recording of his own voice. She hesitated, her gaze riveted to the unconscious back of his head. That head, which once—just once—she had caressed as a lover, holding it between her breasts... Just for a moment, an echo of that terrible yearning which she had felt for him years before reverberated softly through her, as though on a drum. Then she closed the door very quietly and went off to bed.

Hours later, or so it seemed, she came to, to hear a hunting owl hooting outside in the meadows. Her whole body seemed to be on fire and when, more than half asleep still, she pushed back the bedclothes, her skin tingled and smarted. She switched on the bedside lamp and crossly surveyed her reddened arms and chest, looking even more fiery now against the pure white of her broderie anglaise nightie.

She got out of bed and found her toilet bag, although she was quite certain already that she had forgotten, in her haste the previous afternoon, to pack her after-sun cream. She was just climbing back into bed, resigned to an uncomfortable, sleepless night, when she thought, Of course, cold milk—Gran's old remedy for sunburn when she had been a child.

The house was dark; Jude's bedroom door, as she flitted past like a pale moth, was closed. She listened, her ears straining, but no sound reached her; he must be asleep. She reached the foot of the stairs, glanced into the sitting-room—and almost jumped clean out of her overheated skin. The curtains were not drawn and, in the white light of a summer's night, she saw Jude. He was still on the sofa, but sitting upright now, a glass in his hand and a half empty whisky bottle on the low table beside him.

He was so utterly still that she thought he had fallen asleep where he sat, but as she hovered indecisively in the doorway, he must have become aware of her presence, for very slowly he turned his head towards her. His face seemed very pale, his eyes were dark with an expression totally unfathomable. He stared at her without speaking, and feeling a faint twinge of alarm, she advanced a couple of paces into the room.

'Jude, what is it? Are you ill?'

He seemed to rouse himself from a long way away. 'Charley? What are you doing here? I thought you were asleep.'

There was an edge to his voice that made her wish that she had stayed safely upstairs. 'I was, but I came down for some milk.'

He gave a short laugh and gestured towards the bottle. 'If you want a drink, join me.'

His words, though still beautifully enunciated, were faintly slurred, and her uneasiness put a tart edge to her own voice. 'No, thank you. I think you've had enough for both of us.'

He shook his head at her reprovingly. 'Oh, Charlotte, don't be so prim and proper! I'm not that boyfriend of yours. Have a drink.'

'No, thank you,' she replied coldly, stung by his offhand insult. 'For your information, I want the milk for my sunburn.'

Jude leaned forward, switched on the small table lamp and looked across at her. He whistled softly, then pulled a wry face. 'I see what you mean. My fault, I suppose. Look, I've got some after-sun cream somewhere—you'd better have that.' And brushing aside her protests, he went out.

As he had straightened up, something small and light had fluttered unseen from his lap and Charlotte went across to it, stooping with slow reluctance to pick up the photograph. She held it between her fingers, staring again, as Jude must have been doing, at the three of them. Perhaps he too, however fleetingly, had felt the need to remind himself, just once, of that golden time. Unbidden, Cleopatra's chilling phrase which, that afternoon, had leapt off the page into her vision came to her again: 'The bright day is done, and we are for the dark.' She glanced once more at the photograph, then, as she heard Jude's footsteps, hastily tucked it behind one of the cushions.

He came in, holding a large bottle of exclusive after-sun, and she held out her hand. 'Thank you.'

But he held it out of reach. 'I'll do it for you.'

Her eyes widened in alarm. 'No, please, Jude. I'd rather do it myself. It's—it's very sore,' she added lamely.

He frowned, as though to argue, then some of the tension seemed to go out of him. 'All right. But you can sit down and keep me company for a while—and no arguments about that,' as she tried to protest. 'I'm paying for your services, remember, so—— ' he gestured towards the sofa '—sit down.'

They eyed each other for a few seconds, one imperious, one mutinous, then, tight-lipped, Charlotte walked past him and perched on the extreme edge of the chair furthest away from the sofa, trying unobtrusively to arrange the brief skirt of her nightdress to cover as much leg as possible.

Jude threw himself down on the sofa, took a mouthful of whisky, then lounged back, his hands behind his head. She knew his eyes were on her, but hers rested anywhere but on him. The silence grew profound, until she was almost certain that she could hear, not only feel, the erratic beating of her heart. One hand strayed to her neckline and she began agitatedly pleating the white ribbon ties. If this silence between them went on much longer, she was somehow—never mind how—going to have to escape from the room and Jude's oppressive presence, for every fibre in her body was being slowly, excruciatingly, stretched past any bearable point.

'Does Stuart Fletcher prefer you in pretty little white cotton nighties?'

She stared at him, too shocked to speak, and his mouth twisted to a thin line. 'What a waste! Some men would lap that lovely body of yours in silk and satin.'

Charlotte looked down, away from the expression in his eyes, clenching her hands together in her lap, in a vain attempt to stop a trembling which was spreading uncontrollably through her whole body.

'P-please don't talk like that,' she murmured in a low, supplicating voice.

With a huge effort, she leaned back into the chair, partly for support, partly to assume a spurious nonchalance. On the wall behind his head was the phoenix, and she seized on it gratefully. 'I love that picture,' she said tritely. 'Is it yours?'

'Yes, it's a beauty, isn't it?' But he didn't turn his head; she knew he was still watching her. 'I got it last year in Mexico when I was filming there.'

Of course. That Mexican Civil War movie—he'd won an Oscar for his role as a guerrilla leader, betrayed in the end by his love for—— She looked across at him and saw that his gaze had fallen, and he was smiling faintly to himself, his lips seemingly curving with a tender, reminiscent softness. Her eyes widened and she stared at him with new intensity. That actress—Claudia Wexford. She had been his co-star, hadn't she? And surely—yes, that was the film which had run into trouble; even in an age of explicit love scenes, their screen love affair had been filmed with such surging power that one board of censors after another had been rocked back on their heels. And the gossip—Charlotte remembered that too, now—one particular journalist with a syndicated column and almost endless hints along the lines of 'Is this a new Burton-Taylor-*Cleopatra* re-run?' He must be thinking of her now...

A tide of raw, savage emotion ripped through her, almost physically knocking her back into the chair, and her fingers tightened convulsively on the arms. What was wrong with her? Not—oh, God, surely not jealousy? But she couldn't be jealous, not of Jude and a woman—*any* woman—because if she was, it would mean that——

She bit her lip on the appalling, unthinkable thought and, drawn as if by a magnetic force far beyond her control, she slowly raised her eyes. Jude was staring morosely at the carpet; whatever private vision he had been seeing had faded. There were dark shadows under his eyes and round his mouth were lines of fatigue and strain.

She gazed at him, silently fighting with the terrible yearning that, second by second, was growing inside her, to run to him, kneel at his feet, take his face between her hands and kiss away those lines, those shadows. So, after all, she thought with bleak, despairing clarity, the feelings which she had so fiercely told herself were long dead, brutally extinguished by Jude's cruel words on that cold morning in the churchyard, had not died. They had become bitter, grey ashes, which seemed dead but in reality only awaited his return to fan them into scorching, flaming life again, like that phoenix over there. But for her, unlike the golden bird, there could be no joy or exultation, only poignant heartbreak again...

Jude yawned and stretched. He drained his glass, then picked up the bottle of after-sun cream which he had placed provocatively on the table between them, and tossed it across to her.

'Here—you can go.' That shuttered 'Keep Out' sign had come down again, matching his dismissive tone, but as she scrambled to her feet, clumsy with tiredness, he surveyed her pale face. 'You look all in—but there's more of the same tomorrow. I want to work on the earlier scenes again, so I'll need you all day for my lines.'

And lines...and lines...and more lines. Scene after scene, some flowing, some stuttering backwards and forwards between them, Charlotte in turn listening, correcting,

playing the other parts...Iras...Enobarbus...
Cleopatra...

Utterly unsparing, Jude flogged them through the day,
until, by early evening, they were both exhausted. He
went off to shower, while she prepared some cold meat
and salad—they were long past real hunger. Then, the
moment he had finished eating, he got up without a word
and retreated into the other room, clutching his copy of
the text and a sheaf of pencilled notes, closing the door,
with as much deliberation as though he had actually hung
up that 'Keep Out' sign.

Charlotte washed up, then went to shower. It was
almost ten already; she might as well go to bed—her
usefulness for today was clearly over. No doubt, for
Jude, tonight would be a re-run of last night: intensive
work, then a consoling bottle of whisky.

But when she looked out of her bedroom window, it
was still light. Below her, a white, sinuous snake of mist
was writhing along the river, spreading into the lush water
meadows as it went. Some horses were standing at the
water's edge, and as she watched, the mist reached them,
engulfing them, though only to flank height; their backs
and heads were still visible, as though they were
swimming.

Impulsively, Charlotte threw down her nightdress on
the bed. The blue towelling shorts and top she had worn
all day were grubby with dust and perspiration, so instead she slipped into her old white seersucker sundress
which she had rolled up and packed at the last moment
as it would not crease.

Downstairs, she could hear the murmur of Jude's voice
through the door. She slipped out through the kitchen,
crossed the garden, ensuring that she was hidden from
his view if he should be looking—though after all, she

told herself firmly, there was no earthly reason why, her work done for the day, she shouldn't take a pre-bedtime stroll, if she felt so inclined.

She opened the gate and, with a delicious sense of liberation, headed, not down to the river, where she could see *Nereid* lying peacefully, but into the field, wading waist-high through the white opalescence. For some minutes she sat quietly on a grassy mound at the far end, watching the mist below her and feeling the tensions of the previous two days drain away from her—at least temporarily—into nothingness, but then she heard the sound of the gate and Jude was coming towards her.

She watched him approach with a feeling akin to anger. Why had he followed her? Why couldn't he have left her alone? Was he going to vent yet more of his frustration on her, and what form now would his barely pent-up emotions take?

He dropped down beside her and, with no preliminary, said, 'Thanks, Charlotte.'

'For what?' She didn't dare look directly at him.

He put an arm casually across her shoulders, so that she stiffened but then relaxed with a slight feeling of relief. After all, it was at least a gesture of friendliness; maybe, secretly, he too regretted that gulf which lay unspoken between them.

'Oh, for bearing with me. Poor Charley——' weak tears sprang to her eyes at his unthinking use of her pet name and she squeezed them away '—I've given you a rough couple of days.' She turned and he gave her a rueful grin. 'I've heard on the grapevine that I'm considered extremely difficult to work with. I gather Susan—our charming ex-Cleo—refers to me among her mates as "that arrogant bastard".' He shot her an unrepentant smile, then tangled his fingers in a handful of her hair and tugged it gently. 'You'll be glad to get away tomorrow, no doubt.'

But I shan't, I shan't! Charlotte cried silently. I love you, and I may never again in my whole life be as close to you as I am now. She realized that Jude was speaking, slowly, almost hesitantly.

'Charley, I didn't really tell you the truth—well, not the whole truth—about this block with my lines. It's partly because of all my film work, but that's not all. I chose to come back to Stratford—I felt that I had to— but it just hasn't worked out.'

He was staring across the water at something far away, and at the look of empty desolation in his face she impulsively took his hand between both of hers and gently stroked it. But he seemed not to notice.

'It's Simon.' She started violently at the name and Jude looked at her, a wry twist to his lips. 'Oh, don't worry. I'm not about to have another go at you—just at myself. You see, I've never shaken off my own feelings of guilt. I've asked myself a million times, should I have gone off to Italy like that? The ironic thing is that I did it partly, at least, for him. Oh, I grabbed at the chance, I know, but I also thought it would help him. If I disappeared from the scene, maybe he would be able to come out from under my shadow. But instead, his death cast a shadow over *me* that I've never been able to shake off. This season I came back here—a cold, deliberate decision, hoping that it would exorcise the past once and for all.' He frowned, then said bleakly, 'But it hasn't worked, Charley—not at all.'

She was moved almost beyond endurance by the bruised, ravaged look on his face. His words had filled her with intense pain, but somehow she had to put that aside and comfort him if she could. The movement was instinctive, yet, her heart thumping at her own temerity, and terrified that even now he would reject her, she slipped her arm around his neck and turned his head towards her, drawing it unresistingly down to rest against her breast. His thick hair brushed softly against her skin, and she rested her cheek against the top of his head, lost in a bitter-sweet joy and pain.

His breath was warm and she felt rather than heard him breathe her name against her flesh. Then he slowly straightened up and held her away from him, but she looked down, unwilling to meet his eyes.

'Charley?'

There was a wondering question in his voice, and when she did not reply he put a finger under her chin to tilt her face towards him. What she saw in his eyes sent a tremor through her, and when he said again, 'Oh, Charley,' and kissed her softly on the lips, she began to quiver under the almost unbearable sensations.

Jude must have felt the almost imperceptible movement of her body, for the next moment he pulled her roughly into his arms, crushing her to him. This kiss was not gentle, undemanding; his mouth was hard, forcing her lips apart in a devastating intimacy, his tongue sweet in her mouth. She buried her hands in his hair and pressed him even tighter to her as his mouth left hers, sliding down across her throat to linger on the erratically-beating pulse at the base.

She arched her neck in mute acceptance as Jude, his eyes stormy black, looked searchingly at her. She raised her hand to lightly brush one finger across his mouth and, with an inarticulate groan, he tightened his grip on her shoulders until his hands bit into her hot skin. She had been swaying slightly towards him; now he pushed her back on the grass, still warm from the day's unclouded heat, and straightened up, shedding his shorts in one fluid movement. For a second he stood over her, outlined dark against the whiteness that was creeping up on them, and she saw again, fleetingly, that young bronzed god by the swimming pool. Then he sank down beside her, roughly pulling aside her skirt.

There was no finesse, no tenderness. Jude, as though totally possessed by a blazing demon which drove him on with savage urgency, was already moving over her body, possessing her with a raw, potent need that made her gasp with shock. Deep within her, a feeling of pleasure so intense that it was almost unbearable, like a knife wound, began slowly rising, building to some shattering climax, but then Jude gasped out her name again into her shoulder and his rigid, sweat-soaked body collapsed against hers . . .

At last, he raised his head and shot her a wordless, rueful half-smile. Charlotte shook her head and smiled back at him shyly.

'It doesn't matter.' And it was true. A tide was running through her, warming her, suffusing her with happiness and wiping away, for her at least, the cold, barren years of estrangement that had lain between them.

The slow, white blanket of mist rolled across them, closing over their heads, and she shivered in the sudden chill. Jude straightened up and, holding his hands out to her, raised her to her feet so that they stood together in the pale, drifting mist. He put his arm round her waist, pulling her close into his body, and together they stumbled back across the field to the cottage. In the kitchen, he turned her to face him and lifted her hand gently to his lips, his mouth softly, sensuously tracing an erotic spiral round and round her palm until she began to tremble as she felt the matching spiral of desire moving softly within her.

'Sleep with me tonight, Charley.' The command was whispered against her finger, and in response her own hand tightened on his.

In his bedroom, there was still enough light to see by. Jude reached out and carefully untied the two ribbons with which Charlotte had caught up her heavy hair, then gently drew his fingers through it, so that it fell in disorder on her shoulders. Then, just as gently, unhurriedly, he unbuttoned the sundress and eased it down over the slender line of her hips, his hands brushing against her skin so that it tingled under his finger ends. He knelt in front of her, first to lift it from under her feet, then to remove her torn panties, while she stepped out of them like a docile child.

He straightened up again, and surveyed her in silence, as she stood with head bent. Then, 'Has anyone——' there was a long pause, as if he had been going to say something else, then he went on, 'has anyone ever told you how beautiful your body is?'

His voice was low and husky, and she stared at him. How beautiful——? Surely not. No one had ever told her that—in fact, no one had ever had the opportunity to tell her.

'No.' It came as a faint whisper, then as he continued to gaze at her, as though feasting on her nakedness, the soft trembling began deep inside her again.

He gave an angry exclamation and snatched her up, holding her tightly to him. 'Don't be afraid of me, Charley.' His lips twisted. 'I'm not usually such a—brute, I promise.'

Charlotte could feel the self-anger in him, and by way of answer, put her hand up, shyly caressing his tanned chest, her fingers rubbing gently against the fine dark hairs. He lowered her down on to the bed with extreme tenderness, as though afraid she might break, then lay beside her. He propped himself on one elbow and, still quite unhurried, stroked down the length of her body— shoulder, waist, the curve of her hip, her stomach, her thigh—in a movement which, though languorous and undemanding, none the less set little sparks flicking down from each sensitive nerve ending, until she began to feel as though her whole being was concentrated, quivering, along the path of Jude's slowly moving fingers.

At last his hand went to her breast and she half closed her eyes against the image of his long, tanned fingers against her creamy skin, fingers which were gently circling, teasing, until his mouth bent to rouse her nipples to rose-tinted peaks of pleasure. She gave a half-stifled gasp and rolled towards him, but Jude pushed her softly back.

Against her mouth he whispered, 'Sssh! All in good time. We've got all night, remember.' Then, with slow deliberation, his hand moved from her breast down, much further, to rest against the flat of her stomach, his thumb gently stroking the delicate inner skin of her thigh, until her whole body was aching for assuagement. Still, though, he made no other move, and she realised suddenly that not only did he sense her complete inexperience, which somehow she did not mind at all, but also he was saying to her, through his skilled manipulation of her senses, I won't hurry you—this time, I'll wait for you.

His thumb moved, forcing a low moan from her, but as she turned her head restlessly, he said into her hair, 'Take it easy, sweet.'

Take it easy? When she would die if soon he did not release her from this throbbing, trembling fever which had seized her entire body in its grip. She arched against him, tracing her hand down his spine in silent supplication, and as her fingers brushed against the tense muscles under the golden skin of his diaphragm, Jude at last put his arms around her, drawing her to him, fitting her soft curves into the hard lines of his frame, as her body, clenched against life for so long, unfolded before him like one of those tiny, withered scraps of paper which, dropped into a bowl of water, becomes, wonderfully, a delicate flower.

Her fingers tightened on his shoulders and a tide of driving passion engulfed her, a passion so shocking, so terrifying, that it tore her away from everything safe and known. She cried out his name and they both lay still.

CHAPTER TWELVE

CHARLOTTE surfaced from a drowned sleep of oblivion. Jude had not drawn the curtains the previous night; they had slept with the summer moonlight across their bodies, and now the strong light of morning was pouring in.

Very gently, she propped herself up on one elbow to study him at her leisure, something she would not have dared do if he had not been fast asleep still. All the harsh lines had been smoothed away, his mouth was relaxed into a half-smile and the shadows had gone from around his eyes. He moved slightly and a lock of dark hair fell forward over his brow; his long lashes flickered and then fell again as he dropped back into sleep. Like this—vulnerable, his defences lowered, that air of cool irony missing, he looked exactly like the Jude of long ago, from that time before her world had cracked so painfully and she had left Stratford and met——

Stuart. A spasm of guilt shot through her and she lay back, staring at the low-beamed ceiling. I'm not going to marry him, she thought suddenly, and knew that it was true. Perhaps in her innermost heart she had always known it, but consciously she had refused to accept the knowledge, wilfully turning her back on that inner core of being which had clamoured for her attention for so long to tell her that for her it had to be Jude—or no one. What Jude intended for her she did not know, did not even care just now. This moment was enough.

In the meantime, though, he needed another long day on his lines. Charlotte slipped out of bed and, catching up her sundress, tiptoed soundlessly downstairs and switched the kettle on, wriggling into her dress as she waited for it to boil. There was a small mirror above the sink and in it she saw, not her usual pale, composed self, but a stranger's face, pink-flushed, eyes like radiant stars, and lips swollen and pouting from Jude's kisses. She yawned and stretched. All this time, she thought, I didn't know it, but I've been dead inside, and now—like that lovely phoenix—I've come to life again.

Out of habit, she had switched on the television set which stood on one of the units. A breakfast show was on, and just as she was pouring boiling water into the teapot, she heard the interviewer's voice: 'And Cleopatra's a very demanding role. Can you really be ready in ten days, Miss Wexford?'

Charlotte's fingers tensed on the handle. Very carefully, she set down the teapot and stared at the screen.

'Well, it's going to be a lot of hard work, but fortunately I know the part. I played it last year in a campus production as a favour for my old drama tutor.' Claudia Wexford smiled. 'So when Jude rang me——'

'Yes, Jude Renton. At least, it'll be nothing new for you to be playing opposite him. You and he have been— very close—for a long time now, on and off the screen, or so the gossip columnists have it. Although, of course, there has been some talk—on this side of the Atlantic, at any rate—of you two breaking up——'

The actress shook her head vehemently. 'No, you can forget that story—that's just a load of—malicious gossip! Jude and I, we're still—very close, as you put it.'

'It's good to hear you put the record straight, and we have of course also been hearing talk of marriage plans——'

The interviewer paused expectantly, but the actress smiled disarmingly.

'Now, you really can't expect me to comment on that—not at this ungodly hour of the morning, when I've only just flown in from Boston,' she said in her soft New England drawl. 'Let's just say that I wouldn't be totally surprised to be hearing wedding bells in the fairly near future.'

Charlotte wanted to hate her. Beautiful, poised, obviously highly intelligent, with that same totally unconscious aura around her which Jude wore like a badge, somehow setting them apart from ordinary mortals. Yet she couldn't, she thought almost angrily. There was a gentle sweetness, even a faint hint of sadness about the eyes, which against every instinct in Charlotte was making her warm towards the other woman... Her mouth twisted in a grimace of pain. Of course Jude was going to marry her. How could he do otherwise than adore her...?

The interviewer had changed tack again and was now probing on the subject of the forthcoming production, while Claudia Wexford enlarged enthusiastically on her perception of the role. 'I don't intend to portray her as some sort of over-ripe beauty queen, and although I haven't yet had the chance to discuss it with Jude, I don't imagine he'll be playing Antony as a fading playboy in a skirt.'

Charlotte suddenly felt an outsider, a mere onlooker, totally shut out from this side of Jude's world. But didn't he, after all, intend very soon for her to be completely excluded from the whole of his life? And he had not pretended with her, he had not told her that he loved her, lied to her in order to seduce her. She had gone willingly into his arms, because she loved him, but Jude——

The truth leapt at her, naked and horrible, and she gave
a whimper of misery. For him, she was just a part of
the past, one of the shadows which he had needed so
desperately to exorcise, like witchcraft, from him.
Maybe, this weekend, he had set out deliberately to
achieve just that. Well, he had done it now—she knew
by the instinct which had always bound her to him that
he was free and whole again, so could she bear, just at
the moment when her love had flowered into passionate
life again, to have him merely kind; a regretful shrug,
an 'I'll always be very fond of you, Charley, but——'?

'And can we look forward to any nude love scenes to
rival those in *Gods of Fire*?'

Charlotte switched off the set, snatched up her
handbag and fumbled blindly at the door lock. Across
the garden, the sunbeds were still there, the empty glasses
from the cold drink which Jude had fetched them.
Through the gate... not towards the river but up the
hill, along the narrow path, overgrown by tall fronds of
white cow parsley... There was a garage, no doubt
where Jude kept his car. The path became a gravelled
lane that led in turn to a road.

Which way? She was standing, frantically chewing her
lip, when a car pulled up sharply beside her.

'Charlotte?'

At the voice she jumped, then her heart lifted with
pure relief as she recognised the driver.

'*Brian!* I'm so glad to see you. But what are you doing
all this way from Stratford?'

He shot her a curious look. 'Oh, I was dragged out
of bed to cover a rick fire. The police think it's arson.'

He walked round the car, surveying her, and she
became acutely aware of her dishevelled hair and
crumpled sundress.

'Look, Brian, c-could you possibly give me a lift back into Stratford, if it's not too far out of your way?'

'Too far?' That look again. 'Charlotte, love, if you stood on the car, you'd practically see Stratford!'

She got in, his words ringing in her ears. Jude had deceived her—even in this. No, she'd deceived herself, but he had allowed her to believe that she was many miles from town, quite unable to escape.

'Are you all right?'

Somehow she pulled herself together under Brian's puzzled scrutiny. 'Y-yes, I'm fine.'

'Funny. I bumped into Stu and Debbie last night in the Dirty Duck. I somehow got the impression that you were miles away, with some old——' He stopped abruptly, vivid curiosity in his eyes. 'Jude Renton's got a hideaway somewhere round here, hasn't he?' he said casually, and Charlotte felt the bright, guilty flush stain her cheeks.

'Has he?' she replied carelessly. 'Look, Brian, I'm in a bit of a hurry, so——'

'Of course, love. No hassle.' But that speculative look was still there, even when he dropped her off at her front door.

She forced some breakfast down, hoping that tea and toast would magically assuage the terrible pain which seemed to have broken out, quite unlocalised, all over her body. She stared down at the yellow check table-cloth, seeing only Jude's face. Had he woken yet? Was he angry that she had left without a word? No, of course not. He would pour away the stewed tea, make himself some more, and carry it outside into the sunshine, thanking heaven that, her task complete, little Charley had had the good sense and the discretion to—*evaporate*. After all, he'd paid well for all her services, hadn't he, so if a spot of exorcism had been called for—well, it was all in a day's work for Anything Goes.

Charlotte's face crumpled suddenly as tears threatened to spill out. Whatever was she going to do? With a dreadful intensity, she stared at the wall opposite until it seemed to dissolve and she could only see Jude again. She gave a choked, half-fearful sob. She couldn't stay here all day, not in this silent flat—she would go crazy. Somehow she had to drag herself free from these strange, disordered sensations which were threatening to close over her head, drowning her beneath them. But there was one thing at least she could do. She could tell Stuart . . .

He was bending over the desk and spun round in astonishment. 'Charlotte! What on earth are you doing back? What have you done with the old ladies—lost them?'

She pressed one hand to her brow, then, with an enormous effort, said tightly, 'No, it's quite all right, Stu. It's just that they——' She tailed away into silence. He was watching her, frowning in puzzlement. She had to tell him, but how could she bear to inflict on him the same pain which she herself was suffering?

The slatted blind was not properly in place, and to give herself time, time to think and to steel herself, she moved past him to the window, put her hand on the cord—then stood frozen into utter stillness. She watched Jude get out of his car, slam the door with a crash that reverberated the length of the quiet street, then run swiftly up the steps.

The door burst open even as she turned to face him, her shoulder resting against the metal filing cabinet, seeking the support which her legs were all at once refusing her. He had not shaved and his clothes had clearly been dragged on anyhow. She saw Stuart look round, then scowl angrily.

'Renton? What the——?'

But Jude ignored him, as though he had no more reality than an atom of dust in the air, and Charlotte quailed as his eyes, blazing with anger, sought and then held hers.

'What the hell got into you, to disappear like that?'

Charlotte ran her dry tongue round her parched lips. 'I-I'm sorry.'

'*Sorry!*' His voice mimicked her savagely. 'I thought you'd fallen in the bloody river!'

I wish I had. The terrible thought was out, into her mind before she could thrust it from her. This was unbearable—she must end it quickly.

'I thought it was for the best if I left,' she said, very firmly, though she felt as though her heart's blood was being drained from her with every word.

Flinching from the fury in Jude's eyes, her own strayed past him to Stuart, all but forgotten, and she saw, with a jolt of alarm, the dawning incredulity in his face.

'You've been with him for the weekend, haven't you?' His face was a stranger's, ugly and frightening.

'No, Stu. You don't understand. It—it wasn't like——'

But he swept on. 'You almost had me fooled about that night in London, you little——'

He took a step towards her, his hand raised, and she shrank away from him, then Jude's voice, low and dangerous, said, 'Don't touch her, Fletcher. If you so much as lay one finger on her——'

He left the threat unfinished, but Stuart stopped in his tracks. He faced her, his complexion mottled red.

'You cooked this whole thing up between you, didn't you?'

'No, *I* did, Fletcher.' Jude's voice was an insolent drawl, and Stuart spun round to face him.

'Please, Jude, *no*!' Charlotte clasped her hands in entreaty. If Stuart discovered just how he'd been taken for a ride, she was terrified at what he might do—or say. But both men ignored her.

'As you say, it was a con—a couple of actress friends of mine.'

She stared at him numbly, taking in the cold, steely glint in his eye, and her heart sank. Furious at her disappearance, or perhaps it was only angry pride, he was now setting out to be as deliberately provocative as he could.

'But in any case that wouldn't have mattered, would it.' There was a flaying contempt in his voice that made her cringe for Stuart. 'Just as long as the price was tempting enough, that is.'

But Stuart disregarded the calculated insult. Not even looking in the other man's direction, he spat out, 'You couldn't keep your hands off him any longer, could you, you little whore!'

Charlotte gave a gasp and held out her hands as though to ward off his verbal violence. There was a split second of silence, then Jude had crossed the room in a couple of strides and swung Stuart round by the shoulder towards him. He punched him hard on the jaw, a sudden shocking sound in the silence, so that Stuart rocked on his heels against- the desk. Jude stood back, his arms folded, watching him as he tenderly nursed his jaw, where Charlotte could see a puffy swelling already disfiguring the skin.

'I told you—leave her alone. Charlotte was not in on the deception—you have my word on that.'

'Oh come, I wasn't born yesterday, you know.' Stuart's face twisted in a vicious sneer. 'I mean, it's hardly as though she's some pure, immaculate little virgin——' a scream was rising inside Charlotte, and alongside it a terrible, paralysing fear, so that for a few seconds she could only press herself up against the filing cabinet, her hands sweaty against the cold metal '—not by any means. But you know that, of course—or perhaps you don't.' Stuart turned savagely to Jude as her breath almost seemed to bubble in her throat. 'You wouldn't think it to look at her now—that cool, butter-wouldn't-melt-in-my-mouth expression of hers——'

There would be no stopping him now, and she—she could only stand and listen helplessly. '—but our Charlotte has been quite a little goer in her time. When she was seventeen—or was it eighteen? I forget exactly——' Stuart hesitated and for one shuddering instant she thought that he had relented, then '—she had an abortion.'

The ugly word tumbled out into the room like a stone and for a fleeting moment they all three stood as though frozen, then Jude said through his teeth, 'I warned you, Fletcher——'

His balled fist went up, and the action roused Charlotte from her immobility. 'No, Jude, don't!'

She flung herself at him, pulling at his arm. He lowered it and looked full at her, his eyes almost black. 'Don't,' she repeated dully, her shoulders slumping wearily. 'It's true what he says. At least——'

He shook off her retaining arm and seized Stuart roughly by the shoulder. 'Out. *Get out!*'

'No one tells me to get out of my own office!'

'Well, as of now, I'm telling you.' Jude's voice was filled with a barely suppressed savagery that made Charlotte tremble. 'Get out, or I'll smash every tooth in your foul mouth and every bone in your pompous body!'

Stuart shook himself free, shot Charlotte one vicious look and, snatching up his briefcase, went out.

CHAPTER THIRTEEN

THE RAW ugliness of the scene had contaminated her, and Charlotte, clamping her teeth against the physical sickness that was welling up inside her, opened a window as if to let a gust of cleansing air into the room. Like some automaton set working, she began arranging papers on the already tidy desk, her hands jerky and unco-ordinated, but Jude put his hand on her arm, drawing her round, gently enough yet with an irresistible pressure. She saw that two of his knuckles were split right across and blood was trickling down his hand, but he did not appear to have noticed.

'Is it true, Charlotte?' His voice was soft, but there was a disturbing undercurrent to it.

She turned away from him. 'Please—go, Jude,' she said slowly. An intense weariness was settling on her, blotting out everything in a grey cloud of dull misery, but even now it just might be possible to keep the entire truth from him. 'I-I'm very busy.' She went to sit at her desk, but with a suppressed exclamation Jude dragged her back round to face him again.

'I asked you a question, and neither of us is moving until I've had an answer!'

Charlotte raised her eyes slightly, studying his white shirt front. It had been buttoned wrongly, and her hands made a tiny involuntary movement, then sank back by her side. It was not, after all, her place to say, 'Darling, you've buttoned your shirt all wrong.' Someone else would say that. But, even as she told herself that, it was very hard not to lay her head on his chest and let the sorrow overwhelm her... Jude shook her roughly.

'Yes, it's true.' The colourless voice hardly seemed to belong to her. 'At least—I didn't have an abortion. Mum said I must, when Gran sent for her, but in the end I-I had a miscarriage, so everything was—all right.'

Something of the bitter anguish which had racked her through that dreadful night must have communicated itself to Jude, for his grip tightened on her arms, bruising the flesh. She tried to meet his eyes, but her glance fell before the terrifying intensity in his.

'He said you were seventeen, maybe eighteen. I must know—was it Simon's baby?'

A chance. A way out, even at this hour, to protect him. Just one little lie, and her secret would still be safe— safe from doing any more harm to anyone. But she was too late.

'Oh, God, I remember now!' One hand came up under her chin, imprisoning her face, so that she could not look away. Jude had gone very pale. 'When he rang me that last time, he told me he'd asked you to sleep with him. I think he'd begun to feel it was the only way to be sure that you loved him. But you wouldn't.' He gave her a twisted smile. 'We twins did always tell each other everything—well, almost everything——' He broke off abruptly, his eyes dilating, as the full import of his own words suddenly struck home.

He dropped his hands from her and went to stand by the window, looking out through the blinds. 'It was mine, wasn't it? The baby, I mean.' His voice was tight and he was only just in control of it.

Charlotte was staring at his back, then it blurred before her. Fiercely, she blinked the tears away—this was no time for weakness. She must be at her most strong. Jude swung round at her, his eyes bright.

'And that's why you wouldn't, in the end, marry Si, wasn't it?' His mouth, already a thin line, tightened even more. 'You thought you'd be betraying him.' It was a statement, not a question, and she felt her insides vibrate softly with pain at the naked anguish in his voice.

They stared at each other across the expanse of desk, as though they were reading in each other's eyes all the years of sorrow and desolation. Jude shook his head bleakly. 'Oh, God, Charley, what have I done? What have I done to all of us?'

He was leaning against the desk, his head bent, and watching him, she set her mind in a resolve of steel. She had to do just one more thing for Jude. She had to set him free for ever from his burden of guilt.

'No, Jude,' she said urgently, 'you mustn't blame yourself. Simon's death—you heard the doctor say how moody and unpredictable he'd become—drinking too much, more and more.' She took a deep breath. 'I never told him about the baby—and he never guessed, I swear it.' Slowly, Jude raised his head to look at her, and she met his gaze unwaveringly. 'I was with him that last night, remember. It really was all because of his failure as an actor—and you can't blame yourself for that.'

'But you——' the word seemed to be torn from him '—what about you?'

'Oh, Jude!' She forced a careless laugh. 'It was light years ago.' Her heart quivered before his sudden frown, but somehow she willed herself to continue—when he had gone would be the time for her to disintegrate. 'Don't give it another thought. I promise you——' oh God, please forgive my lie, it's for his sake '—I promise you I don't.'

His eyes were fixed on her mouth, as though he was trying very hard to take in what she had said. She flashed him a brilliant smile. 'The two girls I flatted with in London, they'd both had at least one abortion, so——' Charlotte gave an offhand shrug '—a miscarriage is nothing to boast about these days. And now, Jude, you must excuse me.' Her voice was beginning to crack like brittle ice on a frosty morning. 'Something urgent's come up that I need to deal with, so——'

'And what about—last night?' His voice was very careful. 'You're not on the pill, I'm sure of that. Answer me!' he snapped, as she was silent, and she shook her head wordlessly. 'Well then, it happened once—suppose it's happened again?' He was still choosing his words with great precision. 'What will you do?'

What did he imagine she would do? She would have the baby, cherish it, love it, because it would have Jude's eyes, be the tiny part of him that she could keep always. Jude did not love her. Out of some misplaced chivalry, though, he might feel it his duty to—do what? To give up the woman he loved, to bind himself to her . . . ?

She shrugged again. 'Well, I'd just have to deal with it, wouldn't I?'

Somehow she had to get rid of him—now, before this sham self-control splintered into fragments in front of him, as it was threatening to do at any second. She pulled a folder across the desk to her, flicked through it, then abstracted a sheet of paper, holding it up as though studying it, though she could not read a single word.

'I'm sorry, but I really must get down to work now. As for the weekend—well, let's be honest. We both used each other—both exorcised a few ghosts, I mean.'

'And is that all it meant?' demanded Jude, and she felt a faint flicker of anger running through her, warming the frozen misery. What right had he to ask that of her? Perhaps, even now, he expected her to fall at his knees, saying 'No, it meant the whole world, and it will last me the rest of my life—all the while that you're married to Claudia Wexford.'

The anger helped. 'Of course that's all it meant,' she said coolly. 'What else?'

For a long moment they stared at each other, then abruptly Jude swung on his heel. Charlotte stood rigidly by the desk, hearing his footsteps, the car starting up, then roaring away down the street.

Only when all sound had quite died away did she allow her trembling legs to give way. She crumpled limply on to the chair and stared unseeingly at the wall facing her. Jude had gone. Somehow, she must endure this season and then he would be gone for ever. The exorcism had done it's work; the shadows had vanished; there was nothing now to tie him to Stratford with delicate strands of steel. Slowly she laid her head down on her clasped arms and began to cry, terrible, tearless sobs, that wrenched at her whole frame.

After a long while she stood up stiffly, washed her face and hands, picked up her bag and went out, locking the office door behind her.

...into a seemingly endless tunnel of dark days and nights. Days to be got through, somehow, with Stuart so coldly, unremittingly hostile, as though revenging himself on Jude through her, that it was pure relief when he announced that at the end of the year he would be pulling out of Anything Goes, returning to London to a top job with their old firm—and taking Debbie with him. The business was another thing altogether. Charlotte must either put up the considerable amount which he was asking for his half-share, or else, together, they could sell out completely. Either way, it called for clear, hard-headed decisions, which she felt quite unable to rouse herself to make. It was so much easier to let the days drift lethargically on, one succeeding another, buried under a deluge of unremitting work.

But the nights were different. She took the pain, like a physical companion, with her to bed, and woke with it beside her. There was no respite from the demons that invaded her mind, leering out at her from the dark corners of her room as soon as she put out the light. She would lie motionless, reliving over and over again every precious moment of that stolen weekend with Jude, each night despising herself for her weakness, but then, the night after, allowing those bitter-sweet images to engulf her mind once more.

Meanwhile, in a blaze of publicity, *Antony and Cleopatra* had opened. There was, despite all the speculation, no nude love scene, but the serious critics enthused over the two main performances, while the popular papers raved about the electrifying tension that crackled nightly between Antony and his beloved queen, or, as one columnist slyly put it, between Renton and his Wexford...

And then, one Sunday afternoon, just as Charlotte was leaving her grandmother's after her weekly visit, the old lady said, with seeming casualness, 'I had a visitor this morning.'

'Oh?'

'Yes—Jude. He's been to have a look round the Manor. Tells me he's going to take it off the market—he's planning to live there himself.'

Charlotte was aware that she was watching her closely, and bent her head to sniff the sweet peas that had been thrust on her moments previously.

'He had a young lady with him—very nice, she was, even if she is an actress—and a foreigner. He asked me if I'd like my old job back, the cheeky young imp, the one that I had when his dad was a boy—under-nurserymaid. Seems to think he might be needing one soon.' She put her hand on Charlotte's arm. 'Look, love——'

There was no mistaking now the deep concern in her voice. But this compassion, coupled with the raw pain that was surging through her body, was almost too much for Charlotte to bear. She kissed her grandmother quickly on the cheek and retreated to her car.

As soon as she was safely out of sight, though, she stopped. She was alongside the wood which formed the boundary of the Manor, and the longing to wander around the grounds just this one last time before they were barred to her for ever was almost overwhelming. So she had been right. Jude had shaken off the shadows of the past and was free now—free to quit that opulent palace by the Pacific and return to the place which she knew, like her, he had always loved better than any other spot on earth. And he was now free also to bring his bride there.

In the previous days, she had thought the anguish could never be any worse, that it had reached its own finite limits. And yet, as she stared unseeing at that line of beech and oak which marked the frontier of forbidden territory, the sense of loss that gripped her was so intense that she almost thought she might die.

A party of ramblers, booted and rucksacked, passed her, gazing curiously in at her. Their surreptitious glances at last roused her from her stupor and she drove away.

She had not wanted to accept the dinner invitation for the following evening, but the elderly couple she had been chauffeuring around during the last few days had been so insistent that she join them for their final evening before she drove them down to Heathrow the next morning for their flight home to Toronto that it would have been churlish of her to refuse.

She met them in the foyer of the Falcon, their beautiful half-timbered hotel, then they walked down to the Bancroft Gardens for a last stroll, last photographs. Charlotte had taken shots of the couple beside the Shakespeare statue, posed beside Hamlet and Lady Macbeth, and they had then insisted that they take some of her to remember her by. She was standing self-consciously against the backdrop of the river when she heard a too-familiar voice calling urgently, 'Charlotte!'

Startled, she spun round, lost her balance and teetered for a few heart-stopping seconds on the edge of nothing. As she fell towards the green, swift-running water, she fleetingly glimpsed the old couple, mouths open with impotent horror, and then a pair of strong hands had snatched her to safety and she was gazing up into Jude's face.

'W-what did you do that for?' Her voice was shrill with shock. 'You nearly had me in!'

'Well,' the strain in his own features lightened momentarily into a pale smile, 'you can swim, can't you—I taught you, remember?'

She struggled to free herself from his arms, but they tightened around her. 'Charlotte?' His face was very close to hers, his eyes searching her as though seeking something.

'Y-yes?'

'I've got to go now. I'm late already—I've been looking all over town for you. But can I——' he broke off and there was an unaccustomed note of uncertainty in his tone, 'can I come to you tonight, after the performance?'

'Come to me? Tonight?' Charlotte stared at him, almost oblivious to the little knot of interested spectators that had gathered around them. His hand tightened on hers for an instant, as though in reassurance. 'If—if that's what you want.'

'What I want,' there was an urgency in his voice and a message in his eyes which she could not quite decipher, 'is to come back with you right now, but I can't. Look, *Coriolanus* ends at ten-thirty. Give me time to get out of my costume and make-up, I'll be with you soon after eleven. Will you wait?'

For ever, if you want me to. Charlotte nodded.

Jude gathered her to him in a brief, tight hug, then she watched him as he headed in loping strides towards the Theatre.

Using all her professional skills, she got through the meal, smiling and talking in all the right places, but then, as she walked back to her flat through the twilit streets, she at last allowed her mind free rein. Her first spontaneous reaction was a flicker of panic. Why on earth had she agreed for Jude to come to her? After all, she already knew what it was that he was so anxious to tell her. The Manor...Claudia Wexford... Perhaps, for old times' sake, and maybe some slight promptings of guilt, he felt he must tell her personally...

And yet the message in his dark eyes had seemed to be telling her something more, much more. He was offering her one final night of love. But could he really be so heartless, so cruel...? Perhaps she was a better actress than she knew. Perhaps Jude really did believe that for her, too, a casual night's lovemaking, an equally casual farewell over breakfast, was all she sought. Could she bear it, though? Another night in his arms could not satisfy but only intensify the unassuageable longing she felt for him, and leave her yet more empty. She knew, with unblinkered clarity, what the future held for her, and surely her rehabilitation should begin now, not in the morning. It would have been far more sensible for her to have smilingly refused and let him walk out of her life for ever.

But it was too late now. He was coming to her—and she was glad. Tomorrow—what did that matter? But then the memory of the poster that was pinned up on her kitchen wall came to her: 'Remember that tomorrow is the beginning of the rest of your life'. The rest of her life—without Jude. But still she had to take whatever joy this night might offer her. She curled up on the sofa and waited.

She came to, hunched and stiff, and when, fuddled with sleep, she roused herself to look at the clock, she saw that it was two a.m. She straightened up slowly and stared into space for a long time. Jude wasn't coming. Perhaps in her heart she had always known that, in the end, he wouldn't. Finally, he had been too cautious to risk involvement with her yet again. Perhaps—her cheeks blazed at the thought—he had sensed, after all, how she felt about him, and out of some lingering feeling for their childhood closeness had chosen to spare her the anguish which she had been prepared to accept.

As she went slowly through to her bedroom, there was a dreadful, hollow nothingness inside her, as though she were only a tightly-stretched skin. But this numb sensation, almost like the aftermath of a dentist's anaesthetic when one can think but mercifully not feel, was a welcome one. All too soon, she knew, would come the other sensations, closing in on her for the kill.

The telephone roused her. It went on ringing until finally she dragged herself from her bed and answered it.

'Charlotte, is that you?' Debbie's chirpy voice crackled down the line, and she winced.

'What's the time?' she asked.

'Gone eleven. Did you oversleep or something?'

Charlotte made a non-committal sound.

'Well, I thought I'd better let you know that Stu's taking your Canadians down to Heathrow.'

Charlotte closed her eyes and ran her fingers through her hair.

'And you know that group for Warwick and Kenilworth this afternoon? Well, Stu says I can do it, now I've got my driving licence.'

Charlotte knew that she was being shouldered out, but she forced a casual, 'Yes, you do it if you like, Debbie.' A throbbing ache was settling inexorably over her right temple. 'Well, if that's all, I'll——'

'Wasn't it dreadful last night?'

The girl's voice, alive with enjoyment, hardly penetrated.

'Oh?' Charlotte said with weary politeness. 'What?'

'You know—about Jude Renton.'

Charlotte's grip tightened on the receiver. There was—something in Debbie's voice. 'Jude? What about him?' she asked carefully.

'It's awful, isn't it?'

'What's awful? What's happened, Debbie?' Charlotte spoke very clearly, afraid that the terror inside her mind would explode in her voice.

'But surely, you being a friend of his——' there was an undercurrent of awareness in the voice which at another time, in another existence, would have discomfited Charlotte '—we thought you'd know. He's dead.'

CHAPTER FOURTEEN

'AT LEAST,' Debbie corrected herself reluctantly, 'he's dying.'

'Tell me.' The voice belonged to someone else.

'Well, it was nearly the end of the play. He was in a duel, he slipped, and the other actor ran him through, right by the heart.' Charlotte leaned against the wall for support. 'Anne—my friend's mother works at the Theatre. She said it was terrible. He just stood there and the audience thought it was all part of the play, then blood started dripping all over the stage.'

'And then what?'

'When he collapsed,' Charlotte closed her eyes, 'the lights went out and when they came back on, the under-study——'

'Yes,' Charlotte could have screamed at her, 'but what did they do with Jude?'

'Oh, they rushed him round to the hospital, but——'

Charlotte had slammed the phone down and was running, stumbling to her bedroom.

At the hospital, she abandoned the car rather than parking it.

'Can I help you?' the young nursing assistant smiled.

'I-I wanted to enquire about a patient—Jude Renton. Is——?' Charlotte broke off and leaned against the desk, quite unable to finish the sentence. What shall I do? she thought. If Jude is dead, what shall I do with the rest of my life?

'Oh, he's gone, I'm afraid.'

'Gone?' Did she mean——? Charlotte moistened her ashen lips as the girl went on,

'Yes, he was discharged just a little while ago. Well, he discharged himself really, against the doctor's advice.'

Jude was alive! A radiant joy burst inside her, so that she could only stare at the girl.

'But she said not to worry, he'd be very well looked after so——'

'She?'

'Yes, Claudia Wexford. She came to collect him. Oh, she's really beautiful—and those lovely clothes!' An expression of wistful envy flitted across the girl's face. 'She kissed him, then they went out to the car, with her supporting him. She's very fond of him, you could see that—I suppose it's true what all the gossip columns say.'

Charlotte straightened up. 'Thank you. I'm sorry to have bothered you.'

Once back in her car, she sat toying irresolutely with the plastic tag of her key ring, then drove off—not to the office; she simply couldn't endure Debbie's open curiosity—but out into the country for mile after mile. Finally she pulled into a layby high on the hills looking down over Cheltenham and sat, her hands resting limply on the wheel. Was she going to drive on for ever? Once before, she had run away from Stratford because of Jude, but she could not keep on running. Some time she was going to have to turn the car round and head back, to start living again, so in that case, surely the sooner the better.

It was mid-afternoon when she got back to the flat. As she closed the front door she paused, as a strange, disturbing sensation prickled at her senses, momentarily intruding on her misery, but she disregarded it and pushed open the sitting room door. In her frantic haste she had not come in here this morning, and the curtains were still tightly closed. Well, the funeral's over now, she thought, and drew them back. She turned to go through to the kitchen—then stood transfixed.

Jude was sitting on the sofa, his long legs stretched in front of him. Of course. That faint frisson as she had opened the front door, that transient yet overpowering sensation, which she had dismissed, but which would have told her, if she had been prepared to listen to it, that Jude was nearby.

Not able to tear her eyes from him, she put out a hand for the chair opposite him, feeling herself into it.

'H-how did you get in here?' It was the only thing she could think of to say, but he ignored her question.

'Where the hell have you been? I've been waiting for hours!'

Charlotte regarded him closely. Under the suntan, he was extremely pale—alarmingly so. There were black shadows under his eyes and he desperately needed a shave. Suddenly she wanted to put out her hand to him and—— She caught herself up angrily. The shock of seeing Jude, not only alive, but actually sitting—no, sprawling—on her sofa, and clearly not in the sunniest of tempers, had driven all other thoughts from her mind, but now her eyes roamed around the room, as though half expecting Claudia Wexford to appear from no-where, complete with nurse's apron.

'Where is she?' she asked.

'Who, for God's sake?'

'Claudia Wexford, of course.' Then, when infuriat-ingly, he only smiled at her, she added nastily, 'You know—Florence Nightingale the second.'

His smile broadened to a grin and he shook his head at her. 'Dear, dear! Do I detect just the faintest touch of malice, not to say jealousy?'

How could he? How could he toy with her like this? 'Certainly not,' she began hotly, but he waved his hand impatiently to silence her.

'Come over here.'

Charlotte drew back further into the armchair. 'No, I won't.'

Jude swore briefly and violently, made a move to seize her, then his lips tightened on a grunt of pain and he leaned back, his eyes closed. Thoroughly frightened, she sprang up.

'Jude, are you all right?'

'I am perfectly all right,' he said through his teeth, without opening his eyes. 'Just sit down.'

Obediently she sat beside him, seeing that even the careful movement made him wince again. After a few moments, he opened his eyes and managed a pale shadow of a rueful grin.

'I'm better now, Charlotte, truly. They shot me full of painkiller before they let me go, but I've been sitting around so long that it must be wearing off.'

Their eyes met. 'They said you were dying.' Her voice shook.

He pulled a lopsided face. ''Fraid not. To coin a phrase, reports of my death have been much exaggerated.' He reached across and took her hand and, conscious of his discomfort, she let it lie in his. 'Now, where was I? Oh yes, Claudia. You were asking where she is. Well, I should think she's at Heathrow by now.' Heathrow? The whole world was going there today, Charlotte thought inconsequentially. 'After she dropped me here, to await your pleasure, she went haring off for a joyful reunion with Konstantin Astrov.'

'The film director?'

'That's right. The man she's going to marry.'

She gave a great start and turned wondering eyes on Jude, who was watching her, a soft smile crinkling the corners of his eyes.

'But I don't——'

'Ssh.' He put a finger to her lips. 'My poor Charlotte, it's very puzzling, isn't it, but it's all very simple really. You see, for four years I've been nothing but a prize decoy duck. Yes, it's true.' He flashed her a wryly reminiscent smile. 'Claudia's a good friend of mine and I love her very much—and so I'm sure will you when you meet her. But for years she's been madly in love with Astrov. He defected to the West six years ago, but his wife—a physicist—couldn't get out. He's spent years pulling every string he can, cultivating anybody who might help him lean on the authorities. There was no love left, but he and Claudia felt they must get her out if they could, and he knew it would weaken his efforts if it was known that he was having a passionate affair with an American screen goddess.

'So, enter one six-foot decoy duck who just happens to have a secluded hideaway by the Pacific.' Jude grinned with obvious relish. 'I must say, I rather enjoyed getting my own back on the gutter press, for all those years of snide innuendoes. Sometimes, as a great favour, I used to let the pack in for photographs of us two cosily by the pool. You know the sort of thing—Jude Renton and his glamorous mistress?' He glanced at Charlotte interrogatively and she nodded. She knew the sort of thing exactly. 'But what those guys didn't know was that, five minutes after the security gates had closed behind them,

Konstantin had emerged from the woodwork, and the duck, his work done temporarily, was off for a solitary, backpacking weekend in the mountains, disguised in old denims and wrap-around sunglasses.

'The only real scare I—we ever had was that bloody chat show. Whether Hadley was just fishing, or there really were rumours getting around, I don't know, but he was too near for comfort. Anyway, we heard yesterday that Astrov's wife has been granted her visa—she arrived in West Germany this morning. That's why I was hunting all over town for you. I wanted to tell you—just as soon as we knew that she was safely out and the whole wretched charade could end.'

'But—but why? Why was it so important to tell me?'

'Can't you guess?' There was a sudden intensity in his eyes that made Charlotte's breath catch in her throat. He smiled at her. 'Do you really not know how I feel about you?'

'But after the way we parted in the office, I thought you'd never want to see me again. And besides, you—you blame me for Simon's death.'

'As for Simon—yes, all those years I was away I did blame you.' A wry half smile. 'I think I was trying to transfer my own guilt on to you. But the moment I set eyes on you again, I realised it wasn't really him but *you* who'd haunted me all that time. I wanted to hate you, and when, that evening in the garden, I knew I still loved you—that I'd never stopped loving you for an instant— I tried to hate you all the more.'

He took her hand, stroking his thumb gently across it. The ice around her heart was melting; she was breaking free of the straitjacket of misery which had encased her for so long.

'Loving you, hating you, I had to have you near me—hence the *Nereid*. But I thought it had been a disaster. You were on edge all the time—I thought you were missing Fletcher, while I—one minute I wanted to put my hands on your throat, the next I wanted to drag you into my arms and never stop kissing you. After we'd made love, I thought surely, *surely* she'll never go back to him now, but when I woke and you'd gone——' He broke off abruptly, his hand tightening on hers.

'I only left because I saw Claudia on TV—she was being asked about your marriage plans. I couldn't bear it.' Charlotte gave him a tremulous smile.

'Then, when I found out about the baby, I ached to hold you, to comfort you, to make up to you. Ever since, I've been tearing myself in two—desperate to come to you, to prove that what you'd said was just a sham, but I didn't dare. Somehow, out of loyalty to Claudia, I forced myself to keep away from you. I just couldn't risk telling you the truth; you seemed so thick with that reporter, and he'd have a pretty sharp pair of eyes for a world scoop, I reckon.'

And Charlotte, remembering Brian's speculative glances that morning when he'd picked her up, and since then, the various seemingly innocuous phone calls, nodded.

'So I stayed away, terrified that you'd do something stupid like marry Fletcher. I tried dropping a hint to your grandmother, but I don't know if she got the message. It was only yesterday that I was free to tell you, and then I couldn't get to you. This——' he gestured towards the outline of wadding she could see beneath his shirt '—we'd rehearsed that fight a hundred times, but last night I'd got three-quarters of my mind on you.'

A lock of dark hair was flopping over his brow. Very gently, but savouring with an inward glow this entirely new possessiveness, she put out her hand and smoothed it back. Jude moved to take her in his arms, then clutched his side and dropped back against the sofa with a half-smothered groan.

'Don't worry, I'm all right,' as he caught her horrified look. 'They've allowed me out, but with strict instructions that I'm to be looked after—very carefully. But then the nurse I've got lined up abandons me for hours.'

He lifted one hand and lazily brushed it across her lips in a finger kiss. 'Oh, sorry, I forgot to tell you. I'm hiring you to look after me at the cottage.'

Charlotte shook her head at him, her eyes glinting. 'Well, I'm not sure. How long would it be for, do you think?'

'Oh, fifty years at least, I should imagine.'

Her throat was tightening under the suffocating happiness that was filling her from top to toe but she still managed a provocative smile. 'Well, of course, you do realise that in that case it will have to be double rate.'

Jude gave a shout of exultant laughter, then clapped his hand to his side again as beads of sweat broke on his brow.

'The painkillers—they're in my jacket pocket. Get me a couple,' he muttered through set lips.

She hastened to obey, holding a glass of water with unsteady hands for him to sip from, then he lay back with a groan of relief.

'Thanks. I'm afraid they're going to knock me out for a couple of hours, but we can go to the cottage tonight. And if you're a very good girl, I'll let you unwrap me tomorrow and admire my stitches.'

Very slowly, he turned her round to him, and at the loving tenderness and wanting she saw in his eyes, she was filled with such intense joy that she felt dizzy.

'I've waited a long time for you, Charlotte—since you were about three, I think,' he gave her a smile that made her heart melt utterly, 'and I can't wait any longer. I'm going to marry you and live at the Manor again. I want to know,' he went on softly, almost as though to himself, 'that whenever I have to go off filming, you're there, the centre of my life, that I can return to. And, my darling, we will have children, won't we? This time it would be different—I'd be with you.'

Charlotte put a hand to his lips and forced a smile. 'Of course—four at least.' She stopped suddenly. 'And we'll call one Simon, won't we?'

Jude looked at her perfectly steadily and smiled, and she knew with a surge of gladness that the shadow had gone for ever.

His eyes were closing, his mouth relaxing into a sensual tenderness, and she sat beside him, feeling the love that she had held in her heart for him for so long at last burst into unconfined joy... 'Wait for me, Jude...Jude, don't leave me... Oh, come on then, Charley... Jude...'

As she gently lifted his legs on to the sofa so that he could lie full length, he stirred.

'Sorry,' he said thickly, 'I can't—keep awake.'

'Ssh, don't talk.' She put a cushion behind his head. 'Don't leave me——'

He was already retreating far away from her, but she slipped to the floor and sat beside him, her hand in his. He murmured something unintelligible.

'Go to sleep,' she commanded in a whisper. 'I'll be here when you wake, I promise.' I'll be here for always, as long as you want me.

'Charley?' The word was slurred.

'Mmm?'

'Charley—love you...'

You'll flip . . . your pages won't!
Read paperbacks *hands-free* with

Book Mate • I

The perfect "mate" for all your romance paperbacks
Traveling • Vacationing • At Work • In Bed • Studying
• Cooking • Eating

Perfect size for all standard paperbacks, this wonderful invention makes reading a pure pleasure! Ingenious design holds paperback books OPEN and FLAT so even wind can't ruffle pages — leaves your hands free to do other things. Reinforced, wipe-clean vinyl-covered holder flexes to let you turn pages without undoing the strap . . . supports paperbacks so well, they have the strength of hardcovers!

Pages turn WITHOUT opening the strap.

SEE-THROUGH STRAP

Reinforced back stays flat.

Built in bookmark.

BOOK MARK

BACK COVER HOLDING STRIP

10″ x 7¼″, opened.
Snaps closed for easy carrying, too.

Available now. Send your name, address, and zip code, along with a check or money order for just $5.95 + .75¢ for postage & handling (for a total of $6.70) payable to Reader Service to:

Reader Service
Bookmate Offer
901 Fuhrmann Blvd.
P.O. Box 1396
Buffalo, N.Y. 14269-1396

Offer not available in Canada
* New York and Iowa residents add appropriate sales tax.

BM-G

BARBARA DELINSKY

THROUGH MY EYES

Smuggled diamonds...a desperate search for
answers...a consuming passion that wouldn't
be denied...

This May, Harlequin Temptation and Barbara
Delinsky bring you adventure and romance...

With a difference...

Watch for this riveting book from Temptation.

HARLEQUIN
Temptation

"GIVE YOUR HEART TO HARLEQUIN" SWEEPSTAKES

OFFICIAL RULES

NO PURCHASE NECESSARY TO ENTER OR RECEIVE A PRIZE

1. To enter and join the Harlequin Reader Service, rub off the concealment device on all game tickets. This will reveal the values for each Sweepstakes entry number and the number of free books you will receive. Accepting the free books will automatically entitle you to also receive a free bonus gift. If you do not wish to take advantage of our introduction to the Harlequin Reader Service but wish to enter the Sweepstakes only, rub off the concealment device on tickets #1-3 only. To enter, return your entire sheet of tickets. Incomplete and/or inaccurate entries are not eligible for that section or sections of prizes. Not responsible for mutilated or unreadable entries or inadvertent printing errors. Mechanically reproduced entries are null and void.

2. Either way, your Sweepstakes numbers will be compared against the list of winning numbers generated at random by computer. In the event that all prizes are not claimed, random drawings will be held from all entries received from all presentations to award all unclaimed prizes. All cash prizes are payable in U.S. funds. This is in addition to any free, surprise or mystery gifts that might be offered. The following prizes are awarded in this sweepstakes:

(1)	*Grand Prize	$1,000,000	Annuity
(1)	First Prize	$35,000	
(1)	Second Prize	$10,000	
(3)	Third Prize	$5,000	
(10)	Fourth Prize	$1,000	
(25)	Fifth Prize	$500	
(5000)	Sixth Prize	$5	

   *The Grand Prize is payable through a $1,000,000 annuity. Winner may elect to receive $25,000 a year for 40 years, totaling up to $1,000,000 without interest, or $350,000 in one cash payment. Winners selected will receive the prizes offered in the Sweepstakes promotion they receive.

   Entrants may cancel the Reader Service at any time without cost or obligation to buy (see details in center insert card).

3. Versions of this Sweepstakes with different graphics may appear in other mailings or at retail outlets by Torstar Corp. and its affiliates. This promotion is being conducted under the supervision of Marden-Kane, Inc., an independent judging organization. By entering the Sweepstakes, each entrant accepts and agrees to be bound by these rules and the decisions of the judges, which shall be final and binding. Odds of winning are dependent upon the total number of entries received. Taxes, if any, are the sole responsibility of the winners. Prizes are nontransferable. All entries must be received by March 31, 1990. The drawing will take place on April 30, 1990, at the offices of Marden-Kane, Inc., Lake Success, N.Y.

4. This offer is open to residents of the U.S., Great Britain and Canada, 18 years or older, except employees of Torstar Corp., its affiliates, and subsidiaries, Marden-Kane, Inc. and all other agencies and persons connected with conducting this Sweepstakes. All federal, state and local laws apply. Void wherever prohibited or restricted by law.

5. Winners will be notified by mail and may be required to execute an affidavit of eligibility and release that must be returned within 14 days after notification. Canadian winners will be required to answer a skill-testing question. Winners consent to the use of their name, photograph and/or likeness for advertising and publicity in conjunction with this and similar promotions without additional compensation. One prize per family or household.

6. For a list of our most current major prizewinners, send a stamped, self-addressed envelope to: WINNERS LIST, c/o MARDEN-KANE, INC., P.O. BOX 701, SAYREVILLE, N.J. 08872

LTY-H49

Harlequin American Romance

Romances that go one step farther...
American Romance

Realistic stories involving people you can relate to and care about.

Compelling relationships between the mature men and women of today's world.

Romances that capture the core of genuine emotions between a man and a woman.

Join us each month for four new titles wherever paperback books are sold.
Enter the world of American Romance.